DISCARD

THE ART OF LOSING

ALSO BY KEITH DIXON

Ghostfires

THE ART OF LOSING

Keith Dixon

ST. MARTIN'S PRESS NEW YORK

This is a work of fiction. All of the characters, organizations, and events portrayed in this novel are either products of the author's imagination or are used fictitiously.

www.stmartins.com

Epigraph text on page vii reproduced by permission from *The Canterbury Tales* by Geoffrey Chaucer, selected, edited, and translated by A. Kent Hieatt and Constance Hieatt, New York: Bantam, 1981 (second edition).

Library of Congress Cataloging-in-Publication Data

Dixon, Keith, 1971–
    The art of losing / Keith Dixon.—1st ed.
        p. cm.
    ISBN-13: 978-0-312-35868-6
    ISBN-10: 0-312-35868-7
    1. Gambling—Fiction. 2. Horse racing—Fiction. 3. Independent filmmakers—Fiction. 4. Greed—Fiction. I. Title.

PS3604.I95 A88 2007
813'.6—dc22

                                                            2006050972

First Edition: February 2007

10 9 8 7 6 5 4 3 2 1

For Jessica

Perhaps one or two of you
may fall from your horses and break your necks.
Look what a safeguard it is to all of you
that I have fallen in with your company,
since I can absolve you, high and low
when your soul shall pass from your body.

—Geoffrey Chaucer, "The Pardoner's Tale"

THE ART OF LOSING

1

first went to the track right after my third film flopped.
Sebby, my producer, took me. I think he believed the film's
failure was his fault and wanted to help me get my mind off
my troubles and maybe win some cash.

We drove out to Aqueduct on a weirdly hot and bright
March afternoon. After we'd found seats in the grandstand,
Sebby excused himself for ten minutes to go place his bets,
including a fifty-dollar bet he'd conned me into laying on a
horse named Wren's Lament I'd neither heard of nor read
about. When his ten-minute errand became a half-hour disappearance, I began to wish I'd passed on the bet and instead
used the cash to chip away at my gathering credit card debt.
It was enough to be away from the city, enjoying the dazzling
green of the infield, the ivy that curled over the arched windows, the sleazy chatter in the grandstand, the smell of horse
piss and loam, the peal of the bell when the horses burst from

the gate, but as usual I'd picked up the scent of money and done the foolish thing.

Only after Sebby returned empty-handed did I realize that he hadn't made the bets here at the track. He'd been on the phone to his bookie.

"This is good, Mike," he said. "Very, very good."

"You better be right. I need that fifty bucks."

"It's going to be worth twenty-five hundred in a few minutes."

However inviting that thought was, a nagging dissatisfaction remained, a dissatisfaction that was invulnerable to any sort of good news. My third film had tanked, and although the critics had been kind, nothing was going to bring it back. I had been counting on the film getting national distribution, and as usual I went to pieces when it didn't. While you're making it, putting in your twenty-hour days and your sleepless nights, you think, "This will all be worth it when the film hits it big," or, "Everything you've given up will pay itself back twice over after this one screens." And it's exactly these lies you peddle to yourself that kill you when the film tanks. Of the three documentaries I'd made, my second, *Red Circle, Red Square,* was the biggest financial disaster. I leveraged my credit card to get it finished, and when I fell behind on the payments the collection company blacklisted me and shoveled my name to a handful of credit agencies. I unhooked my phone and tried to ignore the notes being tucked under my door. At first these notes said things like, "Due to default," and, "In light of failure to remit." When I received one that began, "To avoid a court hearing," I resolved that I would not call my parents and ask for money. Then I called my parents and asked for money.

I have this thing about money. Somehow I've always equated success with wealth. Or perhaps it's the other way around. This is the result of growing up in the home of a self-made man who started out selling shoe polish door-to-door and ended up with a company of his own, a four-car garage, and an inground pool. My mother, who was born into deeply religious conservative Catholic wealth, was raised to never speak of the vulgar subject of money, which of course only added to my money fixation. Whatever the reason for my hang-up, it worries the hell out of my dad, who never cared much for money, especially now that he has too much of it. He made a pile of cash by accident with a company that makes screws and bolts for government contractors, but he never liked his work. I think he always wished he'd been a painter or a teacher.

When I was young, he always told me, "Mike, I don't want you making the same mistakes I did. Go out and do exactly what you want to with your life. Do something meaningful." So I took his advice and hadn't been out of film school for a year when I realized that being broke all the time was going to kill me.

In my father's mind, being broke meant going to the cheapest cafés and sitting at an outside table wrapped in tweed, sipping clear glasses of *eau de vie* with friends, sharing Gauloise cigarettes and plates of food, and talking about interesting things all the time. Since he'd never experienced being broke himself, even in college, he'd turned to books to learn about it and had read far too much of *A Moveable Feast* and *Winesburg, Ohio* and even some Jack London stories that he'd later tried to push on me. All are good books, but they are dangerous books for a man to read late in life while in the midst of a deeply wistful stage. It was left to me to learn the hard way that being broke meant selling your plasma, counting out the pennies at the bottom of your drawer, and passing up asking out women you really liked because you couldn't afford to take them anywhere. It meant lying to friends when you met them for dinner, telling them that you'd already eaten, when of course you hadn't. It meant going without heat and television and a lot of other conveniences that people took for granted. Some damn fool somewhere got the idea that this enriched the artist's soul, all the denial, but from where I stood it seemed to wither a lot more than it nourished.

When I told my father this, he said, "You're doing what you want. You don't need money."

Tell that to the bank, I wanted to say.

The next Christmas my mother gave me a framed needlepoint that said:

The love of money is the root of all evil.
—I Timothy 6:10

I didn't much appreciate having a wealthy couple tell me that the pursuit of money was peripheral and essentially immoral. "It's not about the money, kid," my father says. "That's because you have so much," I say. "You don't have to worry about it anymore." "You ever smell it, money?" he asks. "Honestly, ever held it right up to your face and had a good, deep breath? It *stinks*. Stinks of impulse, corruption, greed. Stinks of id. It stinks of all those things, but what it stinks of most is the things we had to do to get it. It's not about the money, kid. It can't be."

My friends tell me the same thing. "You're doing what you want," they say. "Be happy for that." Sure, I want to answer. I'm doing what I want. I make films, but I practically have to lay down my life to get twenty thousand dollars from my production company. I make films, but I skip meals because I have to spend the development money on DV tapes, interviews, equipment, and insurance on a car that I can't afford but absolutely cannot move film equipment without. I make films, but I live in a one-bedroom apartment the size of my father's office back home, and I still can't make the rent. I haven't got a television. The plates and glasses in my cabinet are all mismatched. I grind my teeth in bed at night and add sums in my head. I can't take a girl on a date, unless it's a walk in the park. How can I possibly be a success? The biggest problem with the films: no one's seen them. Your friends go to the first screening and pack the house. A few even go to the second screening. Maybe your mother goes to the third. And twenty-five empty screenings later, the film's a tree falling alone in the forest. It never happened. No one saw it, and it never happened.

Sometimes, late at night, I get my blood up and call my father and say, "You had it all wrong. This is all your fault. You should have warned me." He says to me, "People like you are looking to buy something, Mike, except what you want isn't for sale. You think getting more money will make everything all better, but it won't. You'll be just as unhappy as you are now." I told this to Sebby after I'd heard that my third film, *The Daisy Chain,* had ended its New York run. Sebby said, "I'm taking you to the track. We'll win a pile of cash, and then we'll see what's what."

A dark spine of thunderclouds had been hanging overhead to the south since morning and the rain broke as the race I'd bet on roared out of the gate. The bell was still going as the pack curled around the near turn. The horses came around the last turn still in a pack, spreading as they hit the stretch, Wren's Lament in front, all neck and nostril and blurred forelock, every strike of hoof an explosion of water, the horses' heads bobbing forward as the jockeys whaled on them with their crops. The grandstand crowd had come to its feet. "We've got it, Mike," Sebby said, "we've got it, we've got it." He was gripping my arm so hard it hurt, which made me realize I was gripping my race card so hard that my hand hurt. The pack was just pushing to the finish line when our jockey stood up suddenly in the stirrups. The pack passed him and broke the finish line, but neither of us saw it happen. The jockey had slowed the horse to a stop and dismounted, and was standing on the track with the bridle in his fist, holding the horse's bad leg up off the loam and talking gently to him.

We sat there in silence for a long time, the rain already past, Sebby chewing on the brim of his hat and staring unblinking at the mirrored pools that had gathered on the track. I didn't know what to say to console him, and the truth was I was suddenly feeling pretty rotten myself. We'd been so close to a big win. The race was declared official, and we saw on the tote board that Wren's Lament would have paid almost fifty to one.

"I should have bet that other perfecta, Mike," he said.

We went inside and had a drink at the upstairs bar that overlooked the saddling area, but even alcohol couldn't cut through the disappointment. So one vice couldn't ease the pain of another. They piled up on one another instead. I could almost hear my father saying, in his instructive, rich man's voice, "The love of money, Mike, the love of money." At fifty to one, my lame bet of fifty bucks would have paid

off at more than twenty-four hundred dollars, enough to
cover next month's rent and then some. Because my horse
had been out in front so close to the finish, I'd already
counted the money as mine, and when he came up lame, I
felt every dollar of it slip away.

"What was the word on that horse?" I asked.

"The public word," he said, "was that it was still correct-
ing its gait for a strained tendon."

"And the inside word—"

"Was that it had healed up much better than people
thought, and was a sure bet."

"Apparently," I said, "the inside word was wrong."

"Let's go get a bite," Sebby said. "There's someone I
want you to meet."

We drove to a little French place in Greenport, on the
North Fork, where the waiters all had accents and wore
white aprons and the maître d' wore a tuxedo. The menu was
all in French. Sebby bought a bottle of wine that cost almost
a hundred bucks. Though I didn't say so, I thought the
money would have been better saved for his bookie or his or-
thopedic surgeon. The rumors said that Sebby owed money
all over town, and that sooner or later someone was going to
come and break his thumbs.

"Wait'll you try this wine, Mike," he said. "It's a good
Côte-Rôti."

"I can't afford this."

"It's all right," he said. "It's expensed."

I ordered *côte de veau*, which turned out to be a stuffed veal chop. Sebby had grouse that we guessed had been shot that morning in some nearby field. Both were excellent, but we were feeling too down about the horse to enjoy the food much. We were just finishing when a slight man came inside and crossed the room to us.

"Hello, Sebby," he said. "Sorry I'm late."

"Hi, Thierry," Sebby said. "Have a seat, will you?"

He sat between us.

"This is Thierry Vosgues," Sebby said. "Thierry, meet my friend Mike."

Thierry had slicked-back, shiny black hair, and the bluest eyes I had ever seen. He couldn't have been more than five-foot-six, with the build of a quick flyweight boxer, but he had the confidence of a man a foot taller. I took him to be about forty years old. Though he was thin and pale, he didn't seem weak, and I guessed that more than a few men had made the mistake of thinking he was. His nose had been broken at least once, but the lack of symmetry in his face only enhanced his good looks.

"Pleased," Thierry said, and shook my hand. "Do you work with Sebby?"

"Only with Sebby," I said.

"Mike's a genius," Sebby said. "We get him when we're lucky."

"How about you?" I asked.

"Thierry's a jockey," Sebby said.

"It must be nice to be thought of as a genius," Thierry said. "I myself am not."

"Can I get you anything, Thierry?" Sebby asked.

"Some ice water," Thierry said. "I was one hundred and twelve this morning."

Sebby flagged down the waiter and had him bring Thierry a glass of water.

"What will you do when you have to eat?" I asked.

Thierry shrugged.

"Same thing I always do," he said, and tapped the tabletop with his index finger.

"You do that?" I asked.

Sebby had told me that a jockey would sometimes put his finger down his throat to make weight. It seemed like an odd thing for a grown man to be doing.

"That's why I never buy him dinner," Sebby said.

"If you want to make weight," Thierry explained, "you do what you have to. You have to stay light."

"Are you riding this week?" Sebby asked.

"Three sure bets," he said.

"That must be nice," I said.

"Not really," he said. "If you win on a jolly, everyone says, 'Well, it was the horse.' But in a loss it's always the rider who gets blamed. I'd rather ride the rag for the odds-on.

That way you're never anything worse than the loser they already thought you were."

"That's a depressing way of looking at things," I said.

"It's true, though," Thierry said.

He took a pack of cigarettes from his breast pocket, then glanced at the maître d', who nodded to him.

"I don't know many athletes who smoke," I said.

"Smoking keeps the weight down," Thierry said. "It's better than Lasix or amphetamines."

"Even a boxer gets to eat after a fight," I said.

Thierry exhaled smoke through his nose.

"When it comes down to the money," he said, "the owner doesn't want to hear about how good a jockey you are. All he wants to hear is how much weight the horse is going to be carrying."

"What makes you want to ride?"

"My father was a jockey," he said.

So I wasn't the only one. A world full of kids who bought the old man's lines.

"That's all it takes?" I asked.

"It's like Catholic guilt," he said. "It gets passed down whether you want it or not."

"I've heard it's dangerous work."

"Only the steeplechase," Thierry said, and crossed himself.

Sure, I thought. If you really believe that, why are you crossing yourself?

"Listen, Mike," Sebby asked, "you mind if Thierry and I talk some business?"

I did, of course.

"Not at all," I said. "I've got to make a few calls."

I got up from the table. Thierry stood up and shook my hand.

"I hope I'll see you again," he said.

"I'm sure you will," I said.

I went out through the front door and down the dark street without any real idea of where I'd go. It was a lovely night, the smell of spring riding the air, which, in my curious state, seemed to resemble nothing so much as the smell of possibility. With nowhere to go, I walked back to the restaurant, sat on the front steps, and lit a cigarette. I wasn't exactly sure what the business was that they were talking about, but I had a good idea, and I had to admit I was interested. Ordinarily I would have stayed away from something like that, but losing at the track earlier had qualified my sense of what one should and should not pursue. I had the strangest feeling Sebby had known it would.

So here I was again. I'd worked harder on the second film than I had on the first, and harder on the third film than I had on the second. *The Daisy Chain* had cost me one very lonely year of my life. I had spent eight months shooting the daily lives of Bellevue psych ward patients, then another four months figuring out the correct way to link together the seven different stories I'd selected from the raw footage. While others were out living their lives, I was teaching schizophrenics to operate a camera, or listening as two aging obsessive-compulsives argued for the tenth time about the Ping-Pong score. I had made what I was sure was a very good film, and once again it had all come to nothing. No funding for whatever was next, no clear audience. It seemed uncannily appropriate that I'd ended up today at a place that was governed by chance.

Twenty minutes later Sebby came outside and sat down beside me.

"Sorry, old man," he said. "I had to work some things out."

"We'd better head back," I said.

"You want to have a drink first?"

"No," I said. "We should get home."

But neither of us moved. We sat quietly there in the dark, Sebby pensively working through a cigarette, both of us looking out at the street and watching couples glide by, until he said, "It's a sure bet, Mike."

My guns were loaded for this.

"Sebby," I said, "never mind that there's no such thing. Never mind even that. Even if you could get that close to a corrupt jockey, even if you could find one you could trust, one who everyone else trusted and who could keep his mouth shut and who could be counted on to see things through—even if you could do all that, you couldn't make the horse run a step faster. The horse is what it is. There's nothing you could do that would make a horse win that couldn't already win."

"I don't want him to run faster," he said. "I want him to run *slower.*"

I was reminded of the time he'd told me that gambling, in its earliest days, was called "hazardry." How right they'd been, calling it that. This was hazardry, and he was the hazard.

"You get the fastest two-year-old out of the lead," he said. "You get that, and the odds on the quinella go through the stratosphere. Four hundred to one, Mike. I'm not talking about winning a thousand, or even a couple of thousand. I'm talking about winning enough money to change your life. Winning by losing, and using everyone's money against him."

"Thierry won't go through with it," I said.

"He will, Mike."

"You heard what he said about his father. He's too proud of what he does."

"Making weight is killing him. And that's just the day-to-day of it. Imagine the risks he's taking. Sooner or later his number's going to come up, he'll get thrown, and he'll break his neck. He wants to retire, but he's got a wife, two kids, and a mortgage, and he hasn't got enough money to quit. Riding is all he knows. He says to me, 'Sebby, this is the way it's got to be. I worry I'm going to leave my family with nothing.' "

"If you had won today, would you still have come to meet him?"

"Sure," he said. "When you get some, it just makes you want more."

"And you thought you'd share the wealth."

"I thought I owed you, since your reel didn't get picked up."

I didn't believe him. Sebby wasn't a bad person. But he wasn't really a good person, either. As much as I liked him, and as much as I felt I owed him, there was something about Sebby that you couldn't quite trust. He looked out for himself first and last, even when he was working on my behalf, which was a fine quality to have in your producer but a lousy one to have in a friend.

"There's one other thing," he said. "It's kind of tricky, but I was hoping I could trust you, after everything that's gone on between us. I've got a few debts that I haven't paid, so no one's taking any bets from me anymore. Today was my last chance."

"You need me to place the bets," I said. "Thierry wanted to meet me so he could decide if he could trust me."

He knew me so well. All he had to do was hang the cash in front of me.

"These are—these people are different from you and me," he said. "Everyone wants to meet everyone face-to-face before he goes ahead. It's better that way."

"I'd have to think about it."

"Don't think too much," he said. "No one ever got rich off being wise."

We were quiet for a moment. He flicked his cigarette to the curb.

"You remember those guys who ran me out of Los Angeles?" he asked. "They're here, too. They always were. They're running things here in New York, and we don't stand a chance against them, Mike. Guys like Jay Lesch. They can smell the poor on you from five hundred yards. They know it the moment you walk into a room, and they use it to humiliate you. This is not about getting rich. It's about buying back the dignity we both deserve."

I knew what he was getting at. No more skipped meals, no more humiliating myself to his boss. But still making films. Having what I'd always wanted. I might even be able to take a girl on a date.

2

I first met Sebby Laslo at one of those lavish Los Angeles parties where everyone knows what kind of car everyone else drives. This was eight years ago. It was very hot that day and the party was inside. Because I was lucky to be there, twenty-seven years old and green as a Boy Scout, I didn't want to say the wrong thing and disinvite myself, so I spent much of my time outside with the handful of other people who were also lucky to be there. There was a long pool filled with emerald-colored water, an open bar set up on the cement deck, and an ice sculpture of a chimera, with the head of a serpent but the body of a man. I was admiring the sculpture's fangs, watching the points drip and glisten in the sun, and considering the unique difficulties faced by a being who was half-serpent, half-man, when Sebby introduced himself. I liked him immediately. He had that polished look of smoothed hair and perfect tan that Angelenos often use to disguise their sense of moral dereliction. We talked about the projects we were working on. He told me he'd been hired by a major studio to produce a film for their art house division. The film was currently one million dollars over budget, and did I know anyone who could fix a script?

No, I did not.

Very well, then. Did I know anyone who had a pistol handy?

Then he walked away.

The next day I began to ask around about him. Everyone either knew of him or had heard of him, but very few people seemed to know him well. Supposedly Sebby had a divorced father in San Fernando who had suffered a stroke ten years earlier and required constant care and financial support. I had a direct confirmation of this rumor when I met another editor who'd briefly shared an apartment with Sebby in college. He said that all through Stanford Sebby had worked a job on the side, pulling a shift in the evening at a canning factory while everyone else was hitting the beach, and had nearly lost his scholarship when it was discovered he was making money on the side by running a book on the Pacific-10 Conference. The common opinion had been that Sebby would end up either dead or rich by thirty.

We began going out for drinks a few times a week, usually to one or another West Hollywood bar, with Sebby picking up the tab on his corporate card. He made a point of introducing me to everyone he knew. I was flattered by the attention and the access, though privately I feared I lacked the guile necessary to run with such a crowd. He seemed to have the impression that I was an excellent editor. Since we'd never worked together, I guessed that he'd done some digging and had got a report from someone I'd worked for. I didn't learn where he'd got his information until one evening about a month after we'd met. We were at Formosa, and around the time that I lost count of how many drinks we'd had I mentioned that my parents had begun interrogating me about my plans to find a spouse and settle down.

"I'm not surprised," he said. "The entire independent filmmaking community has theories about your marital status."

"Really?" I asked. "Would you care to share these theories?"

"Of course. Some say you're sexually confused."

"I see."

"It could happen to anyone."

"Yes. Even you."

"Others suggest that you haven't enough money to hold a girlfriend."

"They would be correct," I said. "I haven't any money."

"Still others believe you're obsessed with honesty."

"What do you think?"

"I think it's a lost cause," he said, "until you've put Beck out of your mind."

I'd been hired a few months earlier to clean up the workprint of a Danish filmmaker named Beck Trier. Beck had supposedly been forced to fire the previous editor when he began leaving love sonnets written on Post-it notes all over her desk. I really didn't believe the rumor until I met her and fell in love with her myself.

Sebby had slung one arm over the back of the banquette and was watching me with uncomplicated amusement. I looked away, in search of some viable defense, but I found none—because men have no defense against women like that. They hook you from a biological level. Beck could speak five languages. She ran two marathons a year. On the street she was routinely mistaken for a popular underwear model. She was even *nice,* for Christ's sake. I was relieved to hear that she thought I was a good editor.

"Is it so obvious?" I asked.

Sebby shrugged fatalistically and exhaled smoke through his nose.

"It happens to everyone who works with her," he said.

I experienced a sudden panic attack of jealousy. Sebby was better-looking than me, less self-absorbed, funnier. He was quietly confident. At the very least he was much better connected, though I doubted that women like Beck went in for that sort of thing.

"Did you ever work with her?" I asked.

"I should be so lucky."

I was more than a little relieved.

"I've heard you care for your father," I said.

"I do. As best I can, anyway."

"It must be a hell of a lot of work."

"The visits are," he said. "Getting older is really about swapping places with your parents, anyway. They become the kid. But this one, he stares at the wall all day. I walk in the door, he calls me by his dead brother's name. The neighbor says he cries all night. He was supposed to improve a few months after the stroke, but he never did."

Because he'd embarrassed me with the remark about Beck, I felt compelled to needle him.

"Is it true you're a gambler?" I asked.

To my surprise, he blushed and looked into his glass. It was an uncharacteristically vulnerable reaction, and for a moment I regretted asking him.

"Sure," he said. "I guess."

"Why do you do it?"

"A house in Malibu," he said. "Brother, that's what I'm after. Put my dad in the upstairs bedroom, pour myself a drink, and stop running around like a lab rat. I can't keep this up forever."

"I'd get the hell out of here. I'd go to San Diego at least."

"What," he asked, "you don't like it here?"

"I don't know. Do you?"

"Sure," he said. "It's like a big, beautiful nightmare."

It wasn't long until Sebby got run out of town. He'd topped out his corporate card in Las Vegas and had cost the studio more money on top of the budget overrun. Word was that one senior vice president had asked around to see if the police could arrest someone for incompetence. When he found that they could not, he announced that Sebby was banned from the studio for life. I later heard that Sebby had found himself a job at a production company named Axus Films in New York. He was my only good friend in Los Angeles, and though I was happy he'd parlayed himself a second chance, I was terribly sad to see him go. The loneliness that followed was remedied easily enough when I tanked as badly as Sebby and moved to New York less than a year later.

It was nearly midnight when we got back from Greenport. I dropped Sebby off and then ground it out on the side streets for half an hour for a parking space. Back at my apartment I saw that Father DiBenedetto had called twice but hadn't left a message either time, something he did when he wanted to speak to me directly. Father DiBenedetto was not a call-me-back sort of guy. I felt more than a little guilty knowing I'd missed his call because I was at the track and then was meeting with a jockey about fixing a race. He was a good friend, and he didn't seem to mind that I wasn't much of a believer and rarely went to confession. I once said to him, "Father, there's no world but this one," and he said, "Mike, it doesn't matter if you believe in Him or not. What matters is that He believes in you. He'll find his way 'round to you soon enough."

A downbeat, three mechanical clicks, and then a message from Jay Lesch. "Michael," he said, "I've set aside half an hour for you tomorrow, at noon. I'd like you to come by Axus so we can discuss some things." He went on talking, just to hear himself think out loud on my machine. No please, no thank you. Not even a hint at what the meeting was about, or why he'd called it so quickly. Last week I'd pitched him a number of ideas for my next film, so I assumed he was going to give me the green light on one of them, though I doubted I'd get any more development money for this one than I did for the last three. Sebby's boss was a type, all right, a rich bastard with Hollywood looks. His message was exactly the sort of behavior I'd come to expect from him. Sebby sure knew what he was talking about when he was talking about the rich. I hoped he knew what he was talking about with Thierry, too. I pressed DELETE and struck out Lesch's voice midsentence.

Too tired even to brush my teeth, I snapped off the light and climbed under the covers, but once I'd stretched out I found that I couldn't sleep. I'd been warned about Sebby, told that you couldn't count on him to do anything but look out for himself.

How many times had I been told he was a degenerate gambler? How many times had I been told that he had the disease? And how many times had I wanted to answer, "Well, let's think about this. I take a twenty-thousand-dollar development budget against 75 percent profit for the production company. I'm not making thrillers, or chillers, or shoot-'em-ups, or bodice rippers, or buddy flicks, or comedies. I'm making documentaries, the kind of films that ask the viewer to do some thinking. The distributor's got to make all of his cash outlay and his print-and-advertising money back before he makes a dime. A twenty-thousand-dollar budget against 75 percent profit, with national distribution my only hope for a gasp of air. Five or six people take two hours out of their lives to go see something that took me a year of my life to make. And then nothing. Then I do it all over again, and again, and every day I sink a little deeper in debt. So really, I've got to ask you, which of us is the degenerate gambler—Sebby or me?"

I closed my eyes, and in my mind I heard the bell, saw the horses burst from the gates in a tide of rampaging muscle. Here they come. The jockeys whale them with their crops. My pick strains at the front of the pack. I can't look away. Here's the finish.

————

Really, it didn't matter if it was a horse or a film. What mattered was that for every winner there were a hundred who missed by a nose.

Which, if you thought about it, was just code for the time-honored *lost*.

3

The next day I waited in the lobby of the SoHo building
that housed Axus Films until I was exactly ten minutes
late, then rode the elevator up four floors and made my way
through the gloomy warren of white hallways to Jay Lesch's
expansive office. My relationship with Lesch was as complicated as a relationship between benefactor and artist can be,
which is plenty complicated, and I sometimes found myself
being willfully difficult in his presence, if only to shore up
my faltering sense of artistic control. Lesch was at his desk,
talking into his cell phone with visible irritation. He mo-
tioned for me to sit. After a protracted debate about missing
light filters, he collapsed his cell phone, expelled a long-
suffering sigh, and settled his confident gaze on me.

When you sat at Lesch's desk there was no question
which side the money was on. His clothes fit right, and his

watch was the same make and model as my father's. He typically spoke to me as if I were the son he'd never had, dispensing wisdom with weary condescension, and I sometimes found myself wishing he'd have a baby boy with his wife, Gina, so that I might get out from under the weighty yoke of his guidance. His favorite talking point, which was of course unassailable, was that I had failings I didn't know about because I was too young to understand them. This allowed him to lecture without fear of interruption or dissent. As I listened to these lectures, I sometimes found myself thinking that no one ever became wiser—they just got better at what they were good at. And that wasn't the same thing.

"You don't look so good, Mike," he said. "You've got to get some sleep."

He tapped the curry he'd bought for lunch and asked if I wanted half.

"I just ate," I lied.

Lesch was effusive in his respect for my work, especially my first film, and he made every effort to publicly associate himself with me. He did this by inviting me to parties and gallery openings I'd otherwise never have got into, and by making sure we were photographed together for the society papers. I regularly fielded calls from filmmakers Lesch had encouraged to seek my opinion. Since he was my benefactor I went along with all of this cheerfully enough, though I sometimes had to suppress an urge to hand him a bill for my services. I'd had eight years to digest the cruel fact that artistic success did not guarantee financial success. This was what killed filmmakers off. When you're making the thing, you're asking yourself at every step, "Is it right?" because that's the only question that matters. It's the one question you're allowed to ask if you want the film to be any good. But after it's made, there's only one question anyone cares about: Will it sell? If the answer's no, and it usually is, you have to compromise. That was why artists became cynical as they grew older. Cynicism was your only shelter from self-disgust. The compromises all felt vaguely like forays into bad pornography.

Axus was a medium-sized operation that funded, as thinly as possible, a great number of films, the idea being that greater numbers increased the chances of hitting one big. You could generally count on Axus to sign the check if you had a solid reputation. The consequence of this was that with Axus good or very good filmmakers often found themselves lost in a riot of people clamoring for more resources. There was never enough money, and everyone wanted more. We were like the relentless undead in those B-movie horror flicks—always advancing, always pawing at the door lock, with no hope for any outcome but that of getting staked and beheaded by the company's accountants. So why did we keep coming back? Because it was the same grind everywhere else. At least the Axus name legitimized whatever you were doing and would get the attention of the cable networks, the best outlet for a filmmaker nowadays. Since Axus always gave you less than you needed, you were often forced to make up any budgetary difference yourself. Whenever I protested, saying that I couldn't make the film well with the cash Axus had given me, Lesch always said, "Give the network a good treatment and they'll be throwing cash at you." And every time you gave the network a treatment, they told you, "Bring it to us when it's finished."

"You had some praise this week," Jay said.

Sebby had told me I should never believe anything that was written about me, advice I'd managed to follow until I read the final paragraph of *The Observer*'s review of *The Daisy Chain,* where the reviewer made a devastatingly flattering reference to Max Ophuls and *La Ronde.*

"Am I naïve," I asked, "to hope for an ad somewhere?"

He smiled and sat back in his chair.

"You're worried we're not pushing you adequately?" he invited.

"There's nothing wrong with expecting your financial support."

"Appreciate what you have, Michael. You already have more credibility than any of your peers."

"You got Reiner a quarter-million from Searchlight. For a lousy ten-minute pitch he didn't even write."

"Really, Mike, would you want to be Reiner?"

Reiner had a comb-over, bad skin, and a terrible habit of

spilling wine on women at cocktail parties. His leading ladies were always ex-models who required voice coaches. Reiner liked to drive up and down West Broadway in his late-model MG with the top down, even when the forecast was for rain.

"You buy him ads," I said. "He owns his apartment."

Lesch silenced me with a wave of his hand.

"I buy him ads," he said, "because he's a sellout. Money's the only language he understands."

"I can speak money. I can speak dollar, euro, pound, yen, pence."

"Michael—"

"I can speak rupee and ruble and can even read peso."

"Allow me to point out something to you," he said, "something about the pathology of filmmakers, a subject on which I'm somewhat of an expert. Your great grandparents worked themselves to death at jobs they hated, earning enough money so that your grandparents could finish high school. Your grandparents worked themselves to death at jobs they hated, earning enough money so that your parents could finish college. Your parents worked themselves nearly to death at jobs they hated, earning enough money so that you could go to college and then film school. Three and four generations of your family, gathering all its resources, all its willingness to sacrifice, so that you could emerge from film school debt-free and have artistic freedom, a job you love, and a meaningful life. The resolution of generational strife.

Hundreds of your sort darken my door every year, your DNA soaked with historical selflessness. And what do you filmmakers want? What do you want to do with this artistic freedom, this meaningful life? You want to turn it back into money. Like children sent off to play on your own for the first time. The independence frightens you, so you go running back home to Mother. Here, Michael, are the facts. I've funded the development of three of your films. All have screened on both coasts, have gained you positive reviews and public attention, and have caused me to lose money. I've shopped you to every studio and cable network on the planet. I've done this because I have faith in your talent and because I believe that someday you will succeed to a degree that you deserve. We both know how accidental this can be. Until then, you have twice the artistic latitude of anyone on my card. You're the only filmmaker on my card who gets to edit his own material. You're the only filmmaker on my card who gets final cut. That alone is almost unheard of. What more could I possibly give you?"

He was right, of course. No one, absolutely no one, got final cut. Even Beck, before she hit the distribution jackpot two years ago—back when she needed a production company for development. This was the deal I'd insisted on. Sebby, incredibly, had threatened to quit if Lesch didn't come across for me, and he'd won out in the end, though the freedom had cost me dearly. Because you couldn't have both. Everything had its cost.

Lesch pushed the curry across the desk to me.

"Eat this," he said. "I'm happy to share it."

The magnanimous bastard.

"I'm fine," I said.

"Take it," he said. "I can always order more."

I relented and began to eat. Oh, it was good. Lemongrass, scallion, kaffir lime. The heavy-handed spicing brought tears to my eyes. It was too hot and it burned my mouth, but I kept right on eating.

"Sebby's been missing work," Lesch said. "A lot of work. I hear he's been spending time at the track."

"People talk," I said. "You can't trust anything you hear."

"He came in today with a broken thumb and left before lunch. You know anything about that?"

I do, I thought. But I don't think I'll be sharing it with you.

I said that he'd probably had a fall. Jay snorted in disgust.

"He's a good producer," I said.

"When he's here."

"So he's missed some work. He's still made you a pile of money."

"He has. But he's begun to make me look bad."

"You want me to talk to him?"

"No," Jay said, "I want to offer you his job."

I put down my fork.

"You've got to be joking," I said.

"It's a serious offer."

"I couldn't possibly do that," I said.

Lesch shrugged.

"The job is yours to lose," he said. "I was happy with the work you did as a field producer, and I think you'd be right for the slot. We have a history together, and I trust your judgment. But I'd need you soon. As early as next week. I've got a lot of projects lined up."

I began to feel slightly queasy.

"Jay," I said, "what about the ideas we talked about last week?"

"It would just be for a short while," he said. "Until I can find someone permanent. I've got a little too much going on now."

"How long?"

"Six months. A year at the most. Then we can talk about your work."

"Are you saying," I asked, "are you saying—are you telling me you won't produce anything for me?"

"Thanks for coming by," he said. "Let me know by the end of the week."

He stretched out his hand. I took it, of course. I felt like Judas, when he kissed Caiaphas's ring.

The regrettable truth that Lesch had shown the good form not to bring up was that my films weren't getting any better. That, at least, was the collective opinion of the critics, who seemed to think that the films were generally good enough, anyway, though many had begun to devote some ink to wondering where I'd "go" next. I certainly had no idea, and since I'd long since exhausted the goodwill and energy of my various mentors, old film school professors and the like, I had no option but to sift through my material alone and search for the answer there. It is damn near impossible to marshal objectivity when viewing one's own films, and I often found myself, just a few minutes into each screening, out of my chair, pointing at my laptop and loudly refuting some obscure or injurious criticism I'd suffered the previous week.

Of all my films, I hated watching my first one most of all. *Prodigal Son*. It was all simplicity and sincerity, and watching it was like having dinner with an old girlfriend you just knew you shouldn't have split up with. I still marveled at the epic stubbornness and the twenty-hour workdays I'd employed to get the thing made. I had already learned that there was no way around the long hours. Luck is, terrifyingly enough, a big part of the creative process, which is why filmmakers and writers and the like are often more than willing to do nothing but work at their craft from dawn until long past midnight. You have to be at your desk when the inspiration arrives. I have always imagined that I understand just what a farmer feels when he stands on a parched furrow of earth and listens, with jumping blood, to the sound of distant thunder. As an artist you know that what you need is out there somewhere. But it is often given stingily, and according to someone else's schedule.

Prodigal Son was given to me this way, as an accident, which has never been much comfort to me in those barren periods between later projects. It came to me about six weeks after Sebby was banished from Los Angeles. I had been suffering for hours in bed with an ophthalmic migraine, an affliction common to editors, when my downstairs neighbor began to play the *Pathétique* over and over, allegretto, on his piano. *Pathétique* is a lovely thing to hear adagio sostenuto but a lousy thing to hear allegretto, especially when it's late at night and you have a migraine and can't afford anything stronger than aspirin to take the edge off the pain. When he began to cycle through the notes a fourth time, I stomped on the floor in time with the music. Then I hammered on the wall with a paperweight. When the playing continued, I dressed, descended the steel stairwell, and kicked his door until my foot hurt. Instead of playing louder, as I'd expected, the neighbor came to the door, deeply apologetic. He introduced himself as Will Thoreau and asked, somewhat disarmingly, if I was the sort of man to have a drink now and then. I was, I said, but it was very late and I had a terrible migraine. Perhaps another time? No, no, this very minute. It was the least one should do for a neighbor one has kept awake all night.

Thoreau poured me four fingers of bourbon over ice and

drew a glass of water from the tap for himself. I hadn't had anything stronger than beer in weeks and the first sip went down like a burning oil slick.

"You play very well," I said, coughing into my fist. "Are you a professional?"

"You haven't heard of me?" he asked. "I was famous a ways back."

He went to the hall closet and brought out a notebook stuffed with newspaper clippings. A cherubic twelve-year-old Thoreau smiled up from the first page. Apparently he'd been telling the truth—the clippings said he'd composed his first symphony at twelve, and had played Carnegie Hall at fourteen. At fifteen the chair of the National Endowment for the Arts called him "the heir to Shostakovich," and at sixteen Thoreau toured Europe. The clippings ended with a beautiful four-column shot of seventeen-year-old Thoreau onstage at Dvořák Hall in Prague.

"What happened?" I asked.

"I began to hear voices," he said.

By twenty-three, he said, he was too stunned with lithium and haloperidol to compose. The notes dissolved into a string of nonsense on the page or evaporated in his mind before he could get them down. Apparently the madness and the talent sprang from the same well. All he could do now was play.

"What got you started in music?" I asked.

Thoreau shrugged and sipped at his water.

"My father," he said. "He always wanted me to be a composer."

And that was it. With one offhand comment, he hooked me. I spent every free moment of the next six months of my life chronicling Thoreau's decently sad fall from grace. Initial viewings of the raw film confirmed my long-held suspicion that editors made the best shooters. I had initially planned to title the film *The Genius Madman,* but switched it to *Prodigal Son* in what I secretly feared was a cowardly bow and scrape to a new popularity of two-word titles for documentaries. When the workprint was in the can, I asked Beck's production company to back it. They declined. Then twelve other production companies declined, in varying degrees of indifference, regret, and outright hostility. Since I'd invested so much of myself in the film, each rejection felt suspiciously like a rejection of me, and anyone who tried to tell me otherwise was immediately assumed to be working for the enemy camp. I began to contemplate a career in advertising or insurance sales, and realized, to my horror, that I wasn't qualified to pursue either. Two weeks after my twelfth rejection I had a call from Sebby. In the interim I'd developed a bad habit of sitting home all day drinking beer with the shades drawn. I had absolutely no idea what my next move was going to be, and I was hemorrhaging cash. "I'm looking for some new material," Sebby said. "How about that reel you were working on? Is it anywhere close to finished?"

It is no easy thing to leave Los Angeles, though I did it willingly enough when Axus Films hired a sound-mix engineer and offered me ten thousand dollars to shoot additional film, insert some moving stills, and get color correction and online edit. I had never considered the possibility that I might live in New York City, and the adjustment was a hard one. I ordered a set of business cards, hired an accountant, and charged some warm clothes for the coming winter. Sebby had signed on as producer, and Jay Lesch, impressed that Sebby had so quickly signed on someone he'd been assured was a "rising" new filmmaker, gave him a raise. The critics liked the film and were disgracefully lenient about its shortcomings. And I soon noticed that a very pleasant change had occurred: I no longer felt the blood drain from my face when people at parties asked what I did for a living. Most people in the industry seemed to know of me. Though I was neither rich nor famous, I was a filmmaker, and *Prodigal Son* was the proof. I had Sebby to thank for that.

That was what he'd been getting at when he brought up Los Angeles on those steps outside the restaurant. He'd been telling me, however obliquely, that I owed him.

4

Sebby mostly went in for the horses, but when he didn't go in for the horses, he went in for cards. How many times had he dragged me into that casino world, with its nail-biting boredom, its corruption, its busted neon and bad coffee? And how many times, accounting for my own debts, had I waited wearily by the skanked pool, a dog-eared paperback open on my chest, as he gambled away his latest paycheck—how many times? He liked the language of it all, the lingo of horses and cards, the way a junkie liked his mirror, his works, his chopping razor—because language was the paraphernalia of horses and cards. If Sebby was at the track or a poker game long enough, the lingo infected the rhythms of his everyday language. On a walk to pick up cigarettes, you'd hear words like fold, bobble, chute, deuce, overbroke, lady. I'd ask him, "The fuck are you talking about?" A film didn't "fail at the box office," it "boned." An unexpectedly good film was a "Bismarck." A workprint wasn't "nearly finished," it was "on its bell lap."

Five days after my meeting with Jay Lesch, Sebby appeared at my door with a new watch, a fresh shave, and a splint on his thumb. We walked down to the corner of Mercer Street to have a drink, Sebby still in the hyperanimated state of a gambler at the business end of a big run. I had to remind him twice to speak in plain English. I didn't have the heart to tell him the new watch looked a little bit foolish next to his broken thumb, and I didn't think he would have listened if I had. I had decided not to mention that Lesch had offered me his job. He was going on about a run he'd had at blackjack in Atlantic City, how he'd seen counts so high there, so stratospherically high, as to make the toughest riverboat gambler get the cold sweats.

"You get your debts covered?" I asked.

"Every penny. Thank God."

"I suppose you don't need me for the horses anymore."

"I do. They've eighty-sixed me for life. My name, Michael, is mud."

"I'm sure it's not so bad."

"One of them, Popoloskouros—you'll meet him soon, Mike—he put a Greek curse on me."

"I didn't know they had those."

"Oh, yes. *Defixiones*—'prayers for justice.' He has inscribed my name on a lead sheet. Apparently it's quite serious."

"You should think twice about going to Atlantic City," I said. "Sodom and Gomorrah. A bad run there, you're in even worse shape. You should have gone to see your father instead."

"He's getting worse. I walked in the front door last week and he just about jumped out of his skin. He said to me, 'Billy, I thought you were dead,' and I said, 'Dad, it's me. It's Sebby. I'm your son,' but he wouldn't listen. He's convinced I'm his dead brother come back to life. Someday I'm going to give him a heart attack. All because I'm a dead ringer for his brother."

He'd shown me a picture of his uncle once, and I had to agree they looked a lot alike. Sebby's hair had begun to show the faintest signs of thinning, though you could already see that, like his uncle in the photograph, he'd be one of those lucky men who carried his baldness well. He had a long, soulful face and sad eyes the color of smoked glass that attracted the sort of women who liked to help a man get his life together. Sebby was more attracted to the sort of women who disrupted his life, and he considered it a great tragedy that he never could get them because of those eyes. I sometimes thought that a caring woman was exactly what Sebby needed. He had no siblings, no mother, and measured by any reasonable yardstick, no father. With gambling, he was just trying to buy himself good luck. The right woman might be able to cure him of that, or at least fool him into thinking that he'd finally got himself the luck he'd wanted.

"What are you going to do about Thierry, Mike?" he asked.

"I want to try it. I'm not sure what I'm going to do for my share, though."

"You did it again, didn't you?" he asked. "You made the fucking film, and you didn't set any aside for yourself."

"I did," I said, "but I spent it all returning favors."

"You should have saved up, Mike."

"I know it. Don't I know it."

"You could go to your father."

"The hell I could. I wouldn't ask him for a goddamn nickel."

I could feel my face getting flushed already. He'd be so nice about it, and would ask, "How much do you need, Mike?" and I'd say, "A couple of thousand. Maybe three," and he'd say, "Take four, Mike. Take four, just to be sure, and just give back what you don't need. But it's not going to make you happy." And I'd want to ask him, "You think it's happiness I'm after?"

"Don't get upset about it," Sebby said. "I didn't say you *would* go to him. I was just saying you could if you wanted to."

"I wouldn't give him the satisfaction."

"You should give him a chance. He just wants to be friends."

I didn't want to talk about my old man at all right now.

"How much do I need?" I asked.

"Twenty-five hundred."

I looked into my glass.

"That's just to get started," he said. "You're going to need twice that, eventually."

"What for?"

"Because the first twenty-five hundred," he said, "we're going to lose."

I asked him why the hell we were going to lose it. He said I'd understand after I had met Popoloskouros, the bookmaker he wanted to work with. Though in principle he disagreed with the necessity of losing a few hefty bets, there was a need to establish credibility, and nothing established credibility in the gambling world like losing.

"It's like being a filmmaker, Mike," he said. "Any hack can go on making films after a success, but only the ones who've got the disease stick with it through the losses. The more we lose, the less suspicious Popoloskouros will be when we win. And when we win, he'll pay, because he'll secretly believe that eventually he'll win it all back."

Sometimes, he said, if the bookies were feeling suspicious about a win, they wouldn't pay, and then you had to get other people involved.

"This isn't going to get rough, is it?" I asked.

"He's got a temper."

"What happens when he loses it?"

Sebby tapped his splint against the table. The skin beneath was a Weehawken sunset of crimsons and yellows. New watch; broken thumb. That was the gambling life for you.

"Just make sure he doesn't learn that we're friends," he said. "I want this all to work out just right. He broke my thumb. I'm going to break his fucking bank in payback."

I drove to Philadelphia to meet Popoloskouros the next day. He owned a restaurant in Old City, near the wharf. Though the restaurant was just a fence for his bookmaking business, it was a nice place, clean and quiet, with candles on every table and waiters pacing the room in white shirts and ties. The dining room ended at an open kitchen. As I came in the door, a chef raised a cleaver and brought it down with a clean *thuck,* hacking a chop from a raw rack of lamb. When I saw him do that, I felt an almost precognitive certainty that this was all going to be played out again, and under less pleasant circumstances. If the hostess hadn't intercepted me, I might have turned and walked out. I asked if I could speak to Popoloskouros. She went into the back, and a moment later he came out. He was the biggest guy I'd seen in a month, heavy but not fat, reeking of bay rum, with spotless white cuffs rolled down just far enough to cover his jailhouse tattoos. I caught a glimpse of one as he shook my hand.

He asked, in heavily accented English, if I was a reporter.

"I'm down from New York on business," I said. "Can we talk alone?"

He led me to a table in the back and asked the bartender for two retsinas.

"Someone wants to interview you?" I asked.

"We have a reporter who is coming to write a story on the place."

The bartender set two glasses of almost transparent wine before us. I took a sip of mine. The taste was sharp and unpleasant, and the glass chattered slightly as I set it on the table again.

"Tell me your name," he said.

"Jacobs."

"Jacobs. What work are you doing in New York, Jacob?"

"I work with bonds. On Wall Street."

He grinned at me. I could count his teeth, he was so close.

"With a hundred-dollar watch?" he asked. "I'm not thinking so."

I took another sip of wine.

"It doesn't matter, does it?" I asked.

"It must be mattering to you, if you are lying to me. Are you ashamed of what you do for money?"

"I'm a photographer," I said.

It was close enough to the truth that I could say it with a straight face.

"Jacob is a photographer," he said. "For the newspapers or for the galleries?"

"For both."

"One makes money? The other makes art?"

"Something like that."

"Ah," Popoloskouros said wisely. "Let me guess which one is making you the money."

He winked at me.

"The journalism, of course," I said. "I'm like everyone else. I wouldn't do it if I could make money with the other thing."

"So your business is with the newspaper."

"Yes."

"And yet you are here on business with me. You are here on business, because you are wanting to make a pile of money so you can quit the journalism."

His solicitude was beginning to irritate me.

"I want to bet on the horses," I said.

Popoloskouros folded his hands. Though his smile never slipped, for the first time I sensed the presence of the temper Sebby had told me about.

"He comes into my restaurant," Popoloskouros said, "he comes in as nervous as a rookie cop with a wire. He wants to betting on the horses. So why is he not going to the offtrack betting? Why is he not going to the track?"

He was looking directly at me, unblinking. Sebby had coached me on exactly what to say, but he hadn't prepared me for Popoloskouros's calm cross-questioning.

"Same as anyone," I said. "At the track you've got the

limits, the odds, the up-front, the takeout. Not to mention the taxes."

A drop of sweat slipped down my rib cage.

"He wants to bucking the odds," he said. "As nervous as a cop with a wire, he comes to me, in my own restaurant, accusing me of being a bookie. He is such a big shot he doesn't need to be going to the track, with their bad odds, with all their money laid up-front, with their maximum payoffs, with the government taxes. He has no time for such straight dealings."

His glibness had destroyed any faint confidence I had brought with me.

"If I were a cop," I explained, "I wouldn't be so scared."

"Scared," he said. "Why are you scared?"

"I hear you break people's hands."

His grin widened.

"Do you believe that?" he asked. "That I am breaking people's hands?"

"Yes," I said.

"Why do you believe that?"

I told him the truth.

"Because you won't stop smiling," I said.

He sat back and studied me, allowing himself a sip of wine.

"I see you are not wearing a wedding ring," he said. "You don't have a wife?"

"No."

"Why are you down here betting with me? Why aren't you finding yourself a nice girl and settling down? Me, I have my wife to come home to at night. She pours me some wine and rubs my neck and is singing to me. A man needs a woman to come home to at night. All the bad things men are doing in this world they are doing because they have no woman to come home to. When a man has a woman at home, he is going to her and is not out doing foolish things. He is not out causing problems for others."

"You're worried I'm going to cause you trouble."

"Yes."

"Why is that?"

"Because you have no luck. I am seeing that already."

"Then you'll win that much more off me."

He sighed, a tired sigh of days and days lived.

"Do you know why I am agreeing to take your bets?" he asked.

"No," I said.

"Because I know why you are here," he said. "I know you are being sent to me by some degenerate gambler. That is why some square like you is knowing about me, and knowing how to talk to me just right, agreeing with me and agreeing with me like I am a woman you are trying to fuck. He is sending you as a beard, as his cover, because I am not taking any more bets from him, and he is thinking he is going to winning big off me. But the degenerate gamblers never change. They are always losing and losing. I am winning more money off him, except maybe it is money he is not having. So I am giving you a piece of advice, my friend. Have yourself a nice dinner here, on me. It is my way of buying off all the misery you are causing me a month from now, two months from now, when the degenerate gambler you are betting for finds his bad luck has caught up with him. Have the dinner, and then go to your car and drive away and find yourself a nice girl to come home to and do not bet with me. It is the smart thing for you to doing, see? Because when the bet goes bad, it is your hand I am breaking. First your hand, and then I am breaking more until you tell me who the degenerate gambler is, and then I break something of his, except what I am breaking isn't his hand."

His smile was gone.

"Maybe I'd better take that dinner," I said.

I felt like I had spoken through a mouthful of cotton. Popoloskouros reached across the table and patted my hand.

"Smart boy," he said. "You're a smart boy."

I ordered the lamb chops, probably the very same chops the chef had hacked up when I'd walked into the place, but when the waiter set the plate down in front of me I wasn't hungry. I was too sick-scared. Popoloskouros was there in the back, watching me the whole time, so I forced it all down, every bite, then left a twenty for a tip and got the hell out of there.

5

He told you to do what?" I asked.

"To put my hand in the open doorway of his car," Sebby said.

"Couldn't you have called for help?"

"We're at the fucking railyards, Mike. Even the junkies won't go there. And besides," he said, "if you run, it tends to escalate things. You've got no choice."

"So you did what he asked. Then what?"

Sebby lay back on my couch and draped his good hand over his eyes.

"Then he kicked the door shut," he said.

"Listen," I said, "I'm sorry he did that. I'd really like to help you even the score. But I'm not too keen on getting involved with him, whatever the payoff. It's beyond me. I just don't speak that language."

"He really got to you."

"He did," I said. "He was ringing my bells."

"That's how they operate," Sebby said. "They're letting you know up front what's what. To separate the wheat from the chaff."

"Well, it worked," I said. "I'm not cut out for it."

"Trust me with Keegan. Just meet him. He's a different sort. He's from the old school. They don't like violence. They find it distasteful. You might even decide you like him."

"I won't like him when he's kicking a door shut on my hand."

"It won't happen, Mike. Meet him, and you'll see."

Sebby had assured me that fixing a horse race wasn't so difficult if you'd prepared well. We'd wait until Thierry found himself riding the lay horse in a field with a clear win, place, and show. "For the quinella, all we've got to do is call the first two finishers, in any order," he said. "If Thierry takes the lay horse out of the field, and we call the other two, you'll win enough to produce your next film yourself. Every dollar of profit will go into your pocket, not Jay's. If the film gets picked up by a studio, you'll be able to buy a second house in the Caymans." He already had me in a second house, even though I didn't yet own the first.

"Agreeing with me and agreeing with me," Popoloskouros had said, "like I am a woman you are trying to fuck." Sebby knew just how to talk to me and how to provoke me.

It was a confusing time. He'd hinted that I had to do this because I owed him, but I'd begun to wonder if what I really owed him was to not do it. Sometimes you did things because you believed they were the right thing to do, and sometimes you did things because you believed you had to do them. I was still deciding which of the two this was.

Beck Trier called the next day and asked if I'd come to her studio later to check the final cut of her latest film, a documentary about Denmark during the Nazi occupation. The film was slated for online edit in three weeks, and she wanted me to check some slight changes she'd made.

Beck had become one of the independent film scene's most sought-after directors when a major studio picked up her last film two years ago. I went to the debut at the Tribeca Film Festival, and arrived an hour early to a sold out house. I bought myself two eight-dollar glasses of champagne, drained the first while I waited for my change, and slalomed through a cocktail party of creative types dressed in black until I encountered a sound-mix editor I'd worked with last year. He was frowning at the bright screen of his BlackBerry, oblivious to my presence. I read over his shoulder.

From a friend: *Where?*

He, writing back: *TFF.*

Friend: *Yeah but what?*

He, writing back: *Trier's new flick.*

Friend: *How is it?*

He: *Shit. It's shit.*

Oh, sure, I thought. *It's shit.* And not one frame has screened.

What, I often wondered, was the source of this vicious streak, this malignant contempt that divided those of us who should have been most together? The unspoken fact of the New York film scene was that most people would have preferred Los Angeles. Most had even been there at one time or another, and everyone wanted to get back. Making films in New York was much like enjoying a perfectly nice backyard get-together while straining to ignore the sounds of a massive bacchanal taking place a few doors down. At such a moment, one's first instinct is to look around to find someone to blame. The latest film always seemed to present an easy target.

At the screening party that night I never got closer than twenty feet from Beck, as she always had a camera or a microphone in her face. Toward the end of the evening I saw her kissing a handsome actor who'd played, a year earlier, the marked-for-death private in a studio blockbuster about D-day. The next week she received the news that four studios were bidding against one another for distribution rights. She now owned her own production company, Looking Glass, had a full-time assistant, and could get major stars to return her telephone calls. Though eight years had passed since we'd last worked together, we'd remained very good friends. Five years ago, when I heard she was moving to New York, I realized that my interest in her, dormant in her absence, hadn't changed a bit. My wants were modest. I wanted to wake up next to her every morning. I wanted to wash her hair while she reclined in the tub. But I never had a chance. By the time she got around to breaking things off with the latest base-jumping, helicopter-skiing, alligator-fucking hair model she was dating, there were already crowds of brain surgeons and physics luminaries and rodeo stars staking out her apartment. She was never alone.

I walked the four flights up to her studio and found her watering her plants. Beck was famous for her ability to kill every genus, even the toughest bamboo, but each spring she went out and bought a new crop. She referred to the plants as "children," and regarded each inevitable death with a sadness that I sometimes thought was a bit overblown.

"Maybe I shouldn't have given him so much sun," she said, frowning down at a limp amaryllis, a newly crisp fern, a wilted crown-of-thorns.

They all looked as if they had been baked.

"It's the south-facing windows," I said.

Blame removed, she asked me to sit and began to make two cups of the wretched Turkish coffee she was always drinking.

"I saw *The Daisy Chain* last week," she said. "Twice, actually."

"Did you like it?"

"I thought it was wonderful."

"You really did?"

"For Christ's sake, Mike," she said, smiling. "Yes."

The more films you made, the more you realized how precious genuine praise was from another filmmaker.

"I was worried I'd strayed a bit—" I invited.

"You did. Having someone else hold the camera?"

"He had multiple-personality disorder. I never did learn who was doing the shooting."

"It's nice to see you shooting with high-def."

"I bought a DVX100. The 24p is nice. I like the filmic look."

"Bullshit," she said, still smiling. "You shot high-def because you were hoping it would screen in downtown Omaha. You were planning on getting it blown up to 35-millimeter."

And therein the shit I had to put up with from her.

"Call it optimism," I said. "It's something new I'm trying."

"You did your own color correction."

I chewed on my thumbnail for a moment. This was familiar territory. I was known for cutting what I felt were minor corners and shifting the limited development cash to places where it would have maximum impact. In this case, I'd done my own perfectly serviceable color correction so I'd have enough money to do high-definition, which was a mark any serious film had to hit.

"Honestly," she asked, "how much did you save?"

Enough to eat that week, I thought.

The kettle began to boil, and Beck emptied it over the black grounds.

"Enough," I said.

"Your whites were blown out."

"Intentional," I said.

"That's exactly what I say when I'm caught in a mistake."

"Irrelevant."

"Hardly. Point one: if it gets to television we'll all go snowblind."

"I don't think," I said, "there's much risk of that."

She carried two porcelain mugs to the coffee table and sat across from me, her bare feet tucked underneath for warmth. My first impulse was to offer to rub them for her.

"Have you started anything else?" she asked.

"Lesch spiked all my proposals."

"Go elsewhere. You deserve better, anyway."

Filmmakers who had achieved financial success sometimes forgot what it was like not to have leverage. They forgot how easy it was to get left out in the cold, with no financial backing at all. It was nice to know that Beck had such faith in my work, but there were times when that faith seemed a bit misguided.

I sipped my coffee and winced.

"He's offered me Sebby's job," I said. "I think the idea is that I get my next film in trade. No one knows anything about this, of course. He dropped it on me the other day, and I've been avoiding him ever since."

Beck made a clicking sound with her tongue.

"That's tough," she said. "You can't go anywhere else?"

"Axus gives me final cut. They let me edit my own material. If I went somewhere else, I'd have to give all that up. I'd be setting myself back five years."

"But working for Jay, Mike?"

"I could make some good contacts," I said lamely.

She made a derisive sound in her throat.

"Lesch," she said, "thinks Fritz Lang is a disease you get from a Filipina hooker."

"Listen," I said quietly, "I understand how this looks. But I may have to give a little ground this time."

"You're not really going to take it, are you?"

"What choice have I got?"

"You'd better let Sebby know."

"I don't see how I could tell him."

"Bedre åbedbar fjende end utro frœnde," she said.

She'd taught me all the best Danish sayings while we were editing her first film, and I still remembered that one. "Better a friend's bite than an enemy's caress." I wasn't so sure. Sometimes a friend's bite was the kind that hurt the worst.

"You want me to tell him for you?" she asked.

I thought about it.

"I wouldn't want you to get involved," I said.

Beck was weighing the mug with both palms, treating it, as women do, as if its contents were fragile, and I found myself wondering if this was for warmth or for effect. She had a pretty Danish face, with skin that was tanned even in midwinter, and baleful green eyes, but it was her hands that I always noticed, and it was her hands that I always thought about after I'd left her. It didn't matter if she was drinking from a coffee cup, or typing, or knitting. Her fingers were long and slender, and although she took very good care of her nails she never wore rings.

When we met for drinks, an event I managed to engineer at least once a month, she often brought the latest sweater or hat she was working on and would knit while she told me her Hollywood stories. My favorite story of all was one about her scriptwriting partner, Kate Black, who'd awakened one cold night in Los Angeles to find a tarantula in her bed, warming against her hip. Beck was so good with her needles she could knit whole rows without looking down. We must have cut a queer picture, what with her knitting and talking and me listening. Everything she knitted went to her many nieces and nephews with a small tag attached that said, *Det er rigtig koldt udenfor!* ("It's cold outside!") She'd never made anything for me, but every year I held out hope that on Christmas I'd get a package from her, and something inside with one of those tags attached to it.

I sank into a real funk over Beck after I got back from visiting my parents last Christmas. I think it was the time alone in the car that set me off. Time alone can be a great thing if you are a filmmaker sitting at an Avid workstation with a deadline and an obsession, and a truly lousy thing if you are cruising along I-80 with nothing to do but observe the wasted midwinter moonscape of central Pennsylvania.

That evening I became far too drunk and decided that I would write a letter in which I told Beck all the things I felt about her. I scratched the thing out on a notepad over the course of the dying evening but had the good sense to put myself to bed before I got it in my head to fix a stamp to it and mail it off. By morning I forgot what I'd written. After I'd steeled myself with coffee and four aspirin, I read through the pages. The prose careened from honest to ardent to quasi-poetic, with the booze getting the best of me toward the end. Poor spelling, bad grammar. Worse: three exclamation points. Perhaps I'd known all along that I wouldn't mail it and had only wanted to clarify for myself exactly how I felt about her. The letter summed things up nicely. It was no less chaotic and just as incoherent as my desire.

We watched her film, *The Stone Jury,* in silence. I took

notes while Beck knitted beside me, frowning at the screen.
She had cranked up the blues in the color correction, and had
even used what looked like a blue Heliopan filter for some
shots, drenching the entire film in a ravishing, dead-August
shimmer that invested each scene with the vivid quality of a
daydream. Each shot had been carefully placed and coordi-
nated, and I knew that as I was walking home later I'd be seeing the stone streets of Copenhagen baking bright white in
the late-summer sun, the black water of the canal sparkling
beneath the bridges, and the brightly colored flags of the
shipped sailboats snapping in the hard, steady ocean breeze. I
would be seeing the moving-still photograph that showed
King Haakon VII riding his horse alone through the streets
on the afternoon of the Nazi occupation just to prove that he
was still alive, beaten but dignified in his military uniform, his
sword at his hip. I'd be seeing the faces of the Jews Beck had
interviewed, as they described how they'd been ferried to
safety in Sweden. As people described the installation of the
Reichskommissioner, you suddenly became aware of the elo-
quence of those who'd been killed in their beds and weren't
around to tell their part of the story.

When it was over, Beck turned to me with her whole
body and asked if I'd liked it. I noticed that I'd stopped taking notes an hour ago, thirty minutes into the film.

"It's wonderful," I said, and meant it.

"Should I tone it down some?"

"No, no. Don't touch anything."

"Was the blue too much?" she asked.

"Beck," I said, "it was perfect."

She couldn't conceal her happiness, and I could see that she had thought the workprint was perfect and had hoped I'd feel the same way. It was the approval of another filmmaker that you really wanted.

Sometimes when I saw a friend's work that was better than mine, I'd become jealous and wonder why I wasn't able to produce equally good films. It wasn't that way with her, though. Jealousy never entered into it, because I felt I owed her better. Beck was a complicated person, but I believed she meant well in everything she did and couldn't help the small quirks that made her difficult. It was the intensity of her artistic desire, the very thing that sometimes compelled her to keep me at arm's length, that attracted me to her.

"How was the editing, Mike?" she asked.

This was the first film Beck had edited herself, and I couldn't help teasing her.

"Your first film was better," I said.

"Let me buy you a drink. You can tell me all your secrets."

"You have time for me?"

"You should demand a drink for your efforts," she said. *"Svage hjerter vender aldrig skønne piger."*

"What's that one?"

She pulled on her jacket and noosed a scarf about her neck.

"Faint hearts never win fair ladies," she said.

I hadn't enough cash to buy her even a single drink.

"In that case," I said, "I demand two."

We walked five blocks north to a new bistro Beck wanted to try out. She had a weakness for undiscovered gems and would happily slog through ten average meals for the serendipity of an exceptional find. It was a cold evening, and she took my arm as we walked. The restaurant reviews hadn't come through yet, she said, and she hoped we'd be able to get a table outside without a wait. When we arrived there were plenty of tables available, and they gave us a nice one overlooking the street. With a jacket on and the heating lamps overhead we were both warm, and it was pleasant to be watching all the people walking by.

"It's all couples here," I said.

"I wonder why no babies, though."

I wondered why she'd wonder. It was an unusually candid remark for her. Beck was typically reserved and cautious—a survivor, in every sense of the word—sometimes distant, even cold, in the way only a vulnerable person can be. The few men I knew who had dated her in the past still spoke fondly of her, though all offered up in the end that she was something of an ice queen. I just didn't see it. The chemistry seemed to work differently with us.

We had just finished our first round when I spotted
Wendy Blake, a friend I'd met through Sebby, walking our
way with a young couple. Wendy had been a chef since high
school and had worked in some of the best kitchens around
the city. Blake had told me that where he was from—a town
on the south fork of Long Island—names like Trip or Cue or
even Wendy weren't regarded as outlandish. He'd recently
opened a small Pyrenees-influenced brasserie in the East Village, one that I'd heard was doing well.

Wendy spotted me and stopped to talk, then asked if they
could join us. I looked to Beck and watched her roll her eyes
skyward, as if to ask, "Do we have any choice?" With someone like Wendy you did not. The waitress pulled the next
table against ours and Blake and the couple sat down.

"This is Otso," he said. "Otso's a Basque chef. He came
over from Iruña to be my *chef de cuisine.*"

"This is my wife, Reina," Otso said.

"They've been married only six months," Wendy said.
"Who is your girlfriend? She is prettier than the other ones,
Michael."

"My friend. This is Beck Trier. She makes films, too."

Wendy made a great show of kissing her hand. Beck was
amused. "I wasn't aware that they did that sort of thing in
America any longer," she said.

"It's a lovely tradition I'm trying to bring back," Wendy
said. "Do you know what *Otso* means in Basque? If you ask

a Basque chef, he'll tell you *Otso* means 'leek.' If you ask a farmer he'll tell you *Otso* means 'wolf.' But most simply it means 'wild.' "

He held Otso's elbow and looked at me and winked.

Only then did I realize Wendy was drunk.

"I've heard," Wendy said, "that as a young man, Otso had the reputation of being a wolf. But now he's mellowed. Somewhat. Now we can't decide what poor Otso here is. Perhaps he's a leek."

"I am neither a wolf nor a leek," Otso said. "I am a gentleman. It is a certainty."

"I would not marry a wolf," Reina said.

I sensed that Otso was beginning to regret what might have been a reputation he had once enjoyed, and that Beck was beginning to regret accepting Wendy's request to sit down. She shifted her attention to Otso.

"What sort of food do Basques like?" Beck asked. "I've heard that Basque food is the best in Spain."

"Oh, we like everything," Otso said. "We eat sea bream, salt cod, espelette peppers, spider crab, angulas—"

"Tolosa beans," Reina added.

"Idiazábal," Wendy said. "And hearts. They eat hearts."

Beck made a face.

"But surely you eat hearts," Wendy said. "They are wonderful for the constitution, and for the skin. With velvet skin like yours you must have eaten a hundred hearts."

He winked at me again.

"Never," Beck said, laughing. He'd won her over. "Not even on a dare. Why would you eat such a thing?"

"The heart," Wendy said, "is the only way to be sure you've killed something."

"Nothing can survive without the brain," Otso said flatly.

"Yes, yes," Wendy said impatiently. "I was just making a joke."

"It was a good joke," Reina said, "but I'm no longer hungry."

"Are you eating, Michael?" Wendy asked.

"I've already eaten," I said.

This was not entirely a lie, as not two hours ago I'd swallowed an aspirin. Beck had volunteered to buy me a drink, but I couldn't cover a dinner. I'd have got away with the lie if my stomach hadn't snarled in objection.

"Nonsense," Wendy said. "You're not a hair over a buck fifty. You and Sebby both. How is our mutual friend faring? I haven't seen him in a few weeks. He owes me twenty-six bucks."

"Sebby?" I asked. "Someone broke his thumb."

"Right," Wendy said. "Well. I suppose he could be better."

The waitress arrived and Wendy, despite my forceful objections, ordered Beck and me the hangar steak, rare, with shallots. I had no clue how I was to pay for it. For two months I'd been making the minimum payment on my closed-out credit card and had exhausted the goodwill of the bank.

We had a very nice dinner that was privately spoiled for me by the approaching check. I waited for Beck to excuse herself from the table so I could tell Wendy I couldn't cover the bill, but she never left. Eventually, Wendy snapped his fingers at the waitress—only a chef would have the nerve—and made a writing sign in the air. Two minutes later she dropped the bill before Wendy. He picked it up and frowned at the numbers printed there.

"You want to give me cash, Mike?" he asked, still reading the bill.

Reina was showing Beck her engagement ring and explaining the elaborate manner in which Otso had given it to her.

"I haven't got it, Wendy," I said. "All I have is a twenty-dollar bill."

"You want to just use your card?"

"Wendy," I said, "I mean I haven't *got* it."

You'd think I had told him my mother had died, the look that he gave me. I tried to give him the twenty, but he wouldn't take it.

While Otso and Reina were saying good-bye to Beck, he leaned down close.

"I'm sorry, Mike," Wendy said. "I didn't know."

"I'm the one who's sorry."

"Can I help you out?"

I told him I had some things working, and that something was bound to turn up in a few days.

"That's a fucking lie if I ever heard one," he said. "Come by any time. We'll have dinner together at the bar."

"I will."

The three of them crossed through the restaurant, and Beck and I watched them walking west along Rivington Street.

"You want another?" the waitress asked.

We had two more rounds. Beck took the bill, and if she'd heard what I'd said to Wendy, she covered it well.

We said good-bye out on the sidewalk.

"Off to meet someone?" I asked.

I wondered who the latest viscount or Nobel laureate or oil baron was she was dating.

"Back to the studio," she said. "There's no one to meet."

My key ring slipped out of my hand and jangled to the pavement.

"Right," I said, bending to retrieve it. "Thanks for the drinks."

She hugged me tightly, then swiveled and walked south toward Chinatown.

You are about to do something foolish, I thought. Go home and sleep it off before you get it in your head to follow her and say something to her that will do nothing but get you in trouble. Because you don't have the money to back it up, Mike. You have nothing to give her. You're a black hole.

I ascended my flickering stairwell, noting, for the thousandth time, its damp smell of dashed hopes, and went to my phone without turning on the lights.

Sebby answered on the first ring.

I said, "This thing with Thierry."

He never missed a beat.

"Come on over, Mike," Sebby said. "Come over tomorrow, and we'll talk."

6

I drove to Cape May a week later to visit Lad Keegan at his bar. He was much older than Popoloskouros, about the same age as my father, and his voice carried the last faint strain of a nice Irish accent. He ordered me a vodka tonic and a bowl of blue crab soup, the same for himself, saying it was the best crab soup north of the Outer Banks. His cardiologist had been giving him trouble about his cholesterol, he said, but he couldn't bring himself to give up the soup. To make up the difference, he tried never to get upset about anything. His own father had died of a stroke forty years earlier while having an argument with his mother.

"And doesn't she love that," he said. "I say, 'Ma, give the poor devil his due,' and she says to me, 'But Laddie, it's the only time I ever had the last *word*.'"

He had himself a good laugh about that one. Keegan's

driver, a six-foot thug all neck and arms and tattoos peeking out from under his shirtsleeves, was at the end of the bar ignoring us. He seemed bored by the whole affair and was eating a plate of meatloaf and watching a soccer match on the television with the sound turned down. The three of us were alone in the bar.

"You get busy in the summer?" I asked.

"Sure," Keegan said. "We get sailors, fishermen, tourists, drunks."

"You must make a lot of cash."

"You make all you can in the summer."

"In winter?"

"In winter," he said, "you abide."

He took a sip of his drink.

"I'm interested to know how you found me," he said. "I try to keep my books quiet."

"I've got some friends who count cards in Atlantic City."

Keegan laughed.

"That's why I canceled all my card games," he said. "That and roulette. The college kids figured out how to beat the house. Was a day your average bettor was a wiseguy with a bad suit. Now they're all MIT and Harvard sharks in Abercrombie. There's no money in it anymore."

"What do you cover?"

"I cover basketball, baseball, hockey, horse racing."

"It sounds like a lot of work."

"Horse racing is the hardest. A lot of bookmakers have given it up. With football you can put out the Vegas line, but with horse racing you have to know every horse, every jockey running, and then get the odds right. Otherwise you end up in the minus pool. Every other sport, I'm dealing strictly with chalk players, and I can lay off with another bookmaker to cover myself. You can't do that with the horses."

"But you still cover them."

He grinned at me.

"Sure," he said, "for the same reason everyone wants to bet on them. The track is where the money is. That's why you're here. I can tell, because I've been at this so long. You walked in the door, and I said to Clive, this one's a sharp, and he likes the horses. Hey, Clive. What did I say to you when this guy walked in?"

Without looking away from the soccer match, Clive said, "You said he was smart, and he liked the horses."

Keegan opened his hands, as if he'd performed a magic trick. He really thought he was something, figuring me out like that.

"I know your type," he said. "You're too smart for your own good. You look at the horses, at the degenerates who bet on them. You figure you're smarter than all of them combined, and that with a little work you could make a lot of cash and maybe quit your job."

"So," I said, "you've got me pegged."

"Look at you. You've got clean fingernails that are bitten to the nailbed. A nice haircut. You're straight, and you're under pressure."

"That's what the other guy said."

"Which other guy?"

"Popoloskouros," I said. "You've heard of him?"

I had a vague notion that mentioning another bookie would make me seem more legitimate.

"Sure," Keegan said. "Nikos. He's got a restaurant in the Old City."

"I hear he breaks people's hands."

"I hear that, too."

"Do you break people's hands?"

Keegan looked at me obliquely.

"I do what I have to," he said. "It's better when people don't put me in that spot. You won't put me in that spot, will you?"

"I'm too smart to pull something like that."

"Ah," Keegan said wisely. "I know lots of guys who were too smart. And now they've all got broken hands. You know why? Because money changes things."

I fucking hope so, I thought. I was impatient for it to get started.

"I live in New York," I said. "I could drive the money down next week."

"I'll have my bag man stop by. Why don't you give me your address?"

I hesitated.

"Come now," Keegan said. "Do you think I'd take a bet without knowing where to find you? I need some insurance."

"I'm on the corner of Charles and Hudson, under Jacobs. You want me to write it down?"

Keegan shook his head.

"He'll find you," he said.

"How much will you need?"

"That depends," he said, "on how much you want to bet."

"I can put up a thousand next week. Maybe twice that the week after."

Keegan looked me up and down. He was as sharp and as cold-eyed as an insurance salesman, and twice as smart. Everyone who went to a bookie was trying to work some angle, and Keegan was just trying to assign his own risk.

"Listen," he said, "you're a nice kid, so I'm going to ask you something. I'm going to ask if this is really what you want to do. Because once you start laying your bets, you're in, and the only way to get back out is to settle the book. The book's always going to get settled, one way or another. You know what I mean?"

"I understand."

"All right. I'll give you a line of five thousand. That's

your bust-out point. You lose beyond that, we've got to settle the book before I'll take any more bets."

"When do you start breaking hands?"

Keegan finished his drink.

"I see you have a car," he said. "We get to that point, you sign the title over to me, right? Then no one gets his hand broken and everybody goes home happy."

He got up to make some phone calls. I noticed Clive watching me from the end of the bar. His soccer match was still going, but apparently he'd found me the better sport.

"Hey, sharpie," he said. "You know why Lad's so sweet on you?"

I said no, I didn't.

This, I reflected, was a man who understood violence. His knowledge of pain seemed to hang in the air between us. I felt the weight of it.

"Because you're such a dumb motherfucker," he said. "He's sweet on you, because he knows he's going to get rich off you. Your sort, you drive up with your nice smile and your New York haircut and your money hard-on. You think because you have a college degree, you can make it work with the horses. And not one of you has the sense to come in out of the rain. You make a mess, and I'm the one's got to get it sorted out. I can already tell you how it's going to end. It's going to end with you off in the woods somewhere asking me how this happened. Keegan says you're sharp. From where I stand, you look about as sharp as a fucking bowl of soup."

"Thanks for the drink," I said. "I should get going."

"You get going, sharpie."

"Thanks a lot."

"I'll be seeing you, sharpie."

I walked out into the damp night and sat in my car listening to the rain tick on the windshield. I was thinking about all the money we were going to win. Clive wouldn't be seeing me, because we were going to get it right this time. My film had failed, because there was nothing we could do for it but put it out there and hope people went, and of course people never went. But with this we'd get everything correct up front, and since it was all up to us, everything was going to come out our way. Sebby had been right. You only needed to think about the money you were going to win and what the money would do for you after you had it. You only had to prescribe a future for yourself that demanded certain things of the present.

I never met the bagman, because the next day I phoned in our first bet, a sure loser named Kilkelly with a history of doping and a sore cannon bone, and against every odd she won by five lengths. I watched the race at the local OTB in openmouthed disbelief. Sebby and I had chosen her by getting gloriously drunk and throwing darts at the racing papers. Our aim was poor enough, sending a number of darts into the bare wood around the target, but somehow our good luck worked against us and buried the point right in the *e* in Kilkelly. We took one look and were sure we had our loser. Kilkelly got me a five-to-one payoff on a five-hundred-dollar bet, and the permanent nickname of Sharpie with Keegan. Though it killed me to do it, I told him to 'churn' the twenty-five hundred, and place the winnings against my owed five hundred, with the remainder going to credit.

"This is good, Mike," Sebby said. "Now he thinks he's got you on the line. He gets to keep his own money in his hip pocket, and you look like you've got it so bad you don't even have the sense to cash out your first investment."

I said it certainly looked that way to me.

Lesch telephoned early Saturday morning to invite me to dinner. Though he didn't mention Sebby's job, it was understood that I was to give him my final answer on his offer. I considered giving him my answer over the phone, but instead agreed to go, in the hope that he might extend an offer I couldn't refuse or change his mind about backing my projects.

Lesch was on a stepladder in the foyer when I arrived. The room was dark.

"This damn light," he said, and then swore at it again. He was changing the lightbulb. "Every time Gina starts up her hair dryer, we end up in the sixteenth century. It's this

Mickey Mouse wiring. I swear, I'm going to sell the place and move back to Greenwich." When the room was bright again, he said, "That does it."

Gina came downstairs as Jay was carving the foil seal from the wine. We both paused when she entered the room, Gina Lesch being the kind of woman whose presence stopped conversation. She was a radiant Hitchcock blonde, graceful and serene and fifteen years younger than her husband. People often asked me what she was doing with someone like Lesch. The reason seemed clear enough to me: she was with Lesch because he had money. Every accent of her wardrobe was screaming with concentrated, styled cash. Gina was a dead ringer for Kim Novak, with a body that was round in all the right places. Everything about her was soft and sweet-smelling and real as could be, and I'd always thought of her as an example of the possibilities money created. There were certain people that being broke denied you, and Gina was one of them.

"Hi, Mike," she said. "Where's your date?"

"Sick."

"You'll have to be his date," Lesch said.

She turned her attention to her husband.

"Did you fix it?" she asked.

"Did I," he said. "I unscrewed and screwed."

"Sounds like college," she said.

Gina made three courses—clear consommé, steak tartare,

and sole meunière—each as good as something you might have in a two-star bistro. The kitchen had somehow retained its gleaming, bulletproof spotlessness. I had planned to control my drinking so that when the time came I might speak intelligently with Jay, but I was drunk on Gina's perfume and kept drinking Jay's wine, so overwhelmed was I by her presence at my left. By dessert I was seeing double. After we had finished, Jay asked me to walk with him to pick up the early run of the Sunday paper. Gina had already started on the dishes and wouldn't accept help.

"Pick up some cigarettes, will you?" she asked.

We walked to the delicatessen on the corner and bought a paper.

"Have you thought about my offer?" he asked.

Winning money off Keegan had brought everything sharply into focus. Lesch always gave me just enough to tease me into complacency, enough to convince me that I wouldn't be able to do quite as well elsewhere and might as well stay put. This job was just another way for him to get his hooks into me.

"I need some more time," I said.

"I need to know tonight."

"Right now, I've got to say no."

"I had hoped you wouldn't."

"You knew I would, though."

"Sure I did," he said. "That's why you'll never make it in

this business, Mike. You're too caught up in all the things that don't matter. You've got the talent, but you're putting it in the wrong place, and to the wrong end. It's why your films are getting worse."

This stung me more than I let on, because I feared it was true. I'd always secretly believed that my first film was my best.

"The films," I said, "are just as good as ever. The problem is that you're not getting them the attention they deserve."

"Suppose you got distribution," he said. "Suppose you fulfilled your wildest dreams. A picket fence of gleaming statues for your mantle. Then what?"

"I don't know," I said, "I guess then everything falls into place."

"Everything. Explain."

"Wealth. Success. Peace."

Jay shook his head with derision.

"Peace?" he asked. "Mike, dear Mike—do you really think a world that loves you is any less treacherous than one that doesn't?"

From a distance we saw Gina sitting on the front steps. The house was dark. She was drinking a glass of wine and reading a yellowed paperback by the light of the streetlight.

"Don't tell me," Lesch said.

"Flipped on the dishwasher," she said. "Poof. Entire kitchen goes black."

"I suppose you're enjoying this," Lesch said.

"Oh yes," she said. "Very bohemian inside. You don't mind if we sit outside, do you, Mike?"

I said that I didn't.

"You two gents stay put," she said. "I'll return with three glasses."

Lesch and I sat on the steps and watched the people walking by. His remark about my films had stung me badly enough that I wanted to leave, but I needed to find out what his next move would be.

Gina came back out with the wine and asked Jay for a cigarette.

"Would you like one, Mike?" he asked.

"I'll pass, thanks."

I had cut out smoking to save six dollars a day, though I knew it would only be a matter of days before I backslid. I was addicted to nicotine at the subatomic level, a suede-lung junkie strung out on smoke and fire.

"Better that way," Gina said pointedly. "Smoking makes men dead."

"Don't women die, too?" I asked.

"Absolutely never," she said. "Women never die."

"Careful," Lesch said. "You'll end up like Sibyl."

"Who's Sibyl?" I asked.

"Poor girl," Gina said. "Asked Apollo for eternal life. Got it. Forgot to ask for eternal youth."

"Lovely irony," Lesch said.

"The fine print," I said.

"Sorry about your date, Mike," Gina said. "You should bring her to Jay's birthday. We're having a party for his fiftieth."

"A lie," Lesch said. "I'm merely turning twenty-six."

"I'll see if she's free," I said.

"We have to get you married," Lesch said. "No more dating."

"Married's much more fun," Gina said. "Don't you think so, Jay?"

"Of course," Lesch said. "It's like having your own personal electrician."

"The way you talk," she said. "So tough. You want me to have twenty of your babies. I've got your heart on a stick. You're crazy about me."

"I am," Lesch said. "I'm damn fond of you, Sibyl."

I tipped up my wineglass and found it empty.

"Let me get you another, Mike," Lesch said.

He just wanted to hammer away at me and get me to change my mind.

"I have to get going," I said.

"No, you don't," Gina said. "You just want to leave us alone so we can be amorous. Are we embarrassing you by being amorous?"

"I'm never amorous," Lesch said. "Absolutely never. Embarrasses others."

"That's a lie," Gina said. "You were amorous three nights ago." She counted the days on his fingers. "Friday, Thursday, Wednesday. Yes, three nights ago. I'm quite sure of it. Very amorous indeed."

I said again that I had to be going. This time Gina didn't object.

As I was walking down the street I heard them laughing and talking behind me. When I stopped at the corner and looked back, they had already gone inside. I didn't want to think about what they were doing just then. Once you get the image of two people in your head like that, it's damn near impossible to get it out.

Starting the next morning I worked very hard at losing, thinking the bets through, placing my faith in the numbers, figuring which horse was the slowest, the sickest, the oldest, the most used up. In time I perfected a system of negative accountability. It turned out that while the numbers couldn't help you win, they certainly could help you lose. For some reason the numbers worked perfectly in reverse, if you studied them carefully enough. In the end it was just as much work trying to lose as it was trying to win.

I began spending every afternoon at the OTB. My pledge to quit smoking had long since dissolved, so I routinely took smoking breaks at the curb with the rest of the hucksters and hustlers and cheats. I took my time about losing, because it was necessary to maintain the illusion that I was trying to win, and got to know the regulars well. Some of the cheats actually managed to earn a decent living. Owning a Cadillac was the mark of the most successful bettors, and the rare cheat who owned one would keep it parked conspicuously at the curb outside, dropping quarters into the meter and polishing the fenders with the worn fabric of his jacket. Every so often one of these cheats would suddenly show up on foot, and of course then you knew that his luck had turned. You certainly felt sorry for anyone that happened to, though it seemed obvious enough to me that eventually it had to happen to everyone.

The disappearance of a regular was a hundred times worse than the loss of a Cadillac. People would tell me that so-and-so had been picked up for drunk and disorderly or had finally been nabbed for nonpayment of child support, but it was clear enough they were lying and something bad had happened. The missing person would show up a few days later, sometimes with a broken arm, sometimes with a few stitches above an eye. The injuries were never discussed, though they were displayed as conspicuously as the Cadillacs. In a strange way, the respect that was earned was the same for both.

One of the Caddy-losers, a guy with the unfortunate name of Jimmy Mislay, used to pick on me for being so green. I thought he did it to deflect attention from his lost Caddy.

"We ought to get you a shadow-roll, kid," he said.

I asked him what a shadow-roll was.

"A younger horse," he said, "sometimes, when he's running, he looks down and sees his own shadow, and it scares the shit out of him. So the trainer puts a shadow-roll on him, a little lambswool roll that comes halfway up his face, so he can't see his own shadow. That's you, kid. Spooked by your own shadow."

7

Wednesday night I took Wendy Blake up on his offer, and woke early Thursday, exquisitely hungover on Provençal rosé and poorly hand-rolled cigarettes, to my ringing phone. I let it pass to the machine, expecting a follow-up or at any rate a postmortem from Jay Lesch, and covered my head with the pillow when I heard Father DiBenedetto's voice.

"Michael," he said, "I'm sure you already know that this Sunday is Easter, and your mother called to ask if I'd remind you to come to mass. I don't like to lie to her, so I hope you'll show up this year. If you can't come, maybe you could help me move some things out of the sacristy." I lay there with the pillow over my head until he hung up.

When I first moved to New York, Father Kessel, my mother's priest, mentioned a friend of his named DiBenedetto

who ran a church in Manhattan. My mother called Father
DiBenedetto the next day and spoke with him for more than
an hour. He was declared "delightful" and was invited to
protect both me and my soul from urban squalor. Since then,
he'd skulked around in his friendly, tenacious way, buying me
dinner, going to my films, asking me for favors, checking up
on me, and lightly abusing me about going to confession. I
enjoyed all of it but confession, which I skipped at every op-
portunity. I had tried using the "anonymous" confessional,
but it quickly became apparent that my voice and my vices
marked me as clearly as my face. As much as I liked Father
DiBenedetto, the sight of his vestments always provoked a
surge of embedded Catholic dread, the conditioned fear that
had been planted more than two decades ago by Father
Kessel. This fear was for the most part pointless, as Father
DiBenedetto was by far the most likable, relaxed, and secular
priest I'd ever met. The other priests I knew were all
grounded in a school of severity, especially Father Kessel. He
made me read the New Testament back when I was twelve,
every page, and it gave me terrible nightmares. It seemed to
be saying that this world was just a place where you waited
until it was time to face up to God's love, and God's love, as
far as I could tell, was as ruthless as time and a hundred times
as lethal. The way my mother talked about it, you'd think the
Bible was about nothing but love, forgiveness, and peace. The
book I remembered was a bloody mess, with brothers assassi-

nating each other, waves of locusts blotting out the sun, seas of blood drowning the pagans, and the hero just another sucker for a girl—that was what surprised me most about it. In the Book of Matthew, you find out that Christ got in all that trouble because he was trying to impress Mary. She had washed his feet, anointed his brow with olive oil, and done all those other things that are just biblical metaphors for sex. After her brother Lazarus got sick, Jesus left and went to Jerusalem, and Lazarus died while he was away. When Jesus came back, Mary said to him, "Jesus, if you hadn't left, Lazarus wouldn't have died." All the others chimed in. "You can give sight to the blind," they said. "Why can't you keep a friend alive?" Everyone's got his objections, but it was Mary who was ringing Jesus' bells. So he took everyone to the crypt. He rolled back the stone, and said, "Lazarus, come forth."

Lazarus came out alive, but the Bible is silent on what happens to him after that, because Jesus steals the show for the next forty pages. News of Lazarus's resurrection goes straight to the Pharisees, who are afraid that Christ will dazzle them right out of power. They put the matter to Caiaphas, who says, "It is expedient for us that one man should die for the people, and that the whole nation perish not." Then they go to Pilate, and Pontius, frightened of the crowd calling for blood, sends Christ to his doom.

Next thing you know, the Romans have nailed the poor

bastard up. Before sunset, his body is in the crypt, with all the soldiers rolling dice for his coat.

The way I saw it, that was God's love. Even from age twelve I understood what God was about: He loved you, wanted you to be right with Him, and His love was so strong it could kill you. Look what He'd done to His own son, whom He loved better than anyone.

It was during the months that I was reading the New Testament that my father's business really took off. He'd landed a few big government contracts, and because he was afraid to turn down work, he took on a bigger load than he could typically handle. To stay afloat he was forced to work six days a week, leaving for work before I came downstairs for school in the morning, often returning after I'd gone to bed. He was working for the benefit of the family, of course, but to an only child who'd spent the last twelve years enjoying his undivided attention, this change registered as a healthy shock. On my way upstairs to bed I would sometimes pause before the hall closet, where my father's fastidiously hung suits, conspicuously empty, awaited a trip to the dry cleaner. As I looked up at them I would imagine a man whose size and presence greatly outstripped the grinning, unshaven, tired-looking man who woke me every Saturday and Sunday morning by holding my foot in his hand. It was difficult for me to accept that almost all his attention had evaporated, and I missed him terribly. At some point I began to read in this absence a direct affront to my feelings, and decided that the time had come to give him a taste of his own medicine. Since I was young and guileless, I adopted the only tactic I knew to hurt him, which was exactly the one he'd taught me: I became invisible. I stopped leaving notes in his brief-case. At dinner I was sullen and removed. On Sundays, my father's only completely free day and our usual time to-gether, I'd linger alone at the park, fishing in some blighted pool.

My mother, who I had long suspected was psychic, seemed to divine exactly what was happening, and in an im-promptu gift gave me her father's Leica, teaching me, in a single afternoon, how to load the film and use the little ob-long light meter. I found the mechanics of the thing fascinat-ing, and was flattered that she was willing to entrust me with such a sacred object. I began spending my afternoons and weekends walking the footpaths around our house snapping hundreds of photographs of rocks, grass, and trees. I wonder sometimes what the specific appeal of the camera was. Though I was only twelve, my father had already begun pushing those sentimental books on me, and it was gradually becoming clear to me that he held a deep admiration for artists. I some-times think that with each photograph I was trying to snatch back a piece of his love.

I found Father DiBenedetto in the sacristy, moving crucifixes out into the narthex, three ghastly agonies, the real first principle of the thing. They'd been donated by a wealthy friend who had died last week. It gave me the chills just looking at them.

"Don't they bother you?" I asked.

"I think they're beautiful," he said.

"No wonder they won't let you guys marry. Your aesthetics are backward."

He liked that one.

"What's so beautiful about them?" I asked.

"Forgiveness, selflessness, grace. Everything that's hidden from sight."

I told him I couldn't get past the surface aesthetics. It was too much.

"Where will you be this Sunday?" he asked.

"Home," I said, because it was the only answer that wasn't an outright lie. He'd assume I meant home with my parents, while I meant home here in New York, reading the racing papers and plotting another loss.

"That's nice. Your mother says she doesn't see you often."

"My life doesn't follow much of a schedule. It's hard to plan visits."

"When I was your age," he said, "I spent a year in Bombay. Everyone wanted to come visit. So I said, yes, come and visit. But from the moment they arrived, they began to complain. Morning till night they'd ask, Where's the supermarket? Why do I have to boil my water? Why do the streets smell of goat meat? After a while, I told people who asked to visit the same thing. My life doesn't follow much of a schedule, I'd say. It's hard to plan visits. When what I really meant was, I don't want a visit from you."

"She hands Bibles to children in the supermarket. She makes us say grace at a coffee shop. Sometimes it's a little much for me."

"Perhaps if she saw you more," he said, "she wouldn't need it so badly."

He certainly had me there.

"Did you see my film?" I asked.

"Last week. At the Film Forum."

"Did you like it?"

"Not so much my thing, really," he said. "Which takes nothing away from it, I hope."

I didn't mind. His honesty was disarming, and he was right. Our sensibilities were just too different.

"My parents ask about it," I said. "My mother says she's going to drive to the city to see it."

"I told her she ought not to. I worry she'll be frightened by it."

"She'll tell me I'd make a better film with God's help."

"I admit," he said, "that your mother's manner of thinking can sometimes be dangerous. She thinks that God is always the entire solution."

"You don't think so?"

"He's half the solution to every problem. It's up to the conscience to cut out whatever's left."

We nailed the crosses up and checked that they were level. I thought they looked every bit as ghastly in the angled light of the narthex, but I didn't say so. Father DiBenedetto seemed extremely pleased and asked if I'd join him for lunch. Though it was after three o'clock, I wasn't about to turn down a free meal. It wasn't lost on me that for all I'd won from Keegan I was as broke as ever.

We walked up Prince Street and got ourselves a table at Kelley and Ping's. In the back, across the open kitchen, gouts of steam and smoke rose to the rafters. It was strange having lunch with a priest. Father DiBenedetto talked about his time in Bombay. Everything there was hidden, he said, in a dark and malignant beauty, and you had to develop a new way of seeing if you didn't want to get overwhelmed by it all.

He insisted I try the Moo Yang, a plate of grilled pork with sticky rice. I noticed that he hadn't bothered to pick up a knife and fork.

"You use your hands," he explained.

The first bite was so good it brought tears to my eyes. We

had a nice time, though I knew he'd go home afterward and call my parents to say that I was doing well. He'd find out that I hadn't really been honest about going home, but that couldn't be helped. I figured if anyone had the means to forgive a lie, it was Father DiBenedetto.

8

Sebby's apartment stank of money, that dejected, basement smell of damp one-dollar bills cycled a thousand times through the cheat system. My father had been right in that much, at least.

"You get a call from Clive?" he asked.

How long, I wondered, could we hold this together? We were like sailors bound together and thrown overboard. Adrift and tethered in fathoms of debt. If you kept your head, if you controlled the panic and worked together, you made it. And no one ever did.

Why not take more? I thought. Thierry's just another jockey, and Sebby's the invisible man. That seems like an awfully good deal for them, and a lousy enough deal for you.

I lit a cigarette and sat watching its trembling tip, thinking of gambling, of hazardry, and its hazard of debt. The sharks at

the OTB called it the "railbird affliction." This stress of living a life in the red. Those sharks—they earned more money
per year than brain surgeons. They also paid out more money
per year than brain surgeons. They swore and begged, im-
ploring the dodgy gods of luck and money, and all the while
debt went quietly about its work, doing its subtraction thing.
Five thousand dollars was the distance between me and nothing, between me and zero. Clive had called to remind me of
what I already knew—that I owed money. And I didn't have
my end. He was coming to see me, I owed him, and I didn't
have my end.

"We went through last night," I said.

"That's good. That's what we wanted."

I got up and began to pace the room.

"It's what you wanted," I said. "I'm the one he's calling."

"I don't blame you for being scared."

"It's not your neck on the chopping block. It's easy for
you to break the book when it's not you Clive's coming to
see."

"You've got to relax."

"I haven't got what I owe. I've only got your half."

"He's not going to get rough on the first call. It takes
months for that stuff to kick in. It's a hassle for them, and a
risk, and no one wants it to come to that. You've got nothing
to worry about. Why don't you sit down?"

I sat down, but got up again a moment later. If you sat still for too long, you began to think of all the things they could do to you. There were so many ways they could hurt you.

"I wish I'd never got in this," I said.

"You're coming at it all wrong. This is what we planned. We're exactly where we wanted to be."

"It's different now that it's here."

"Listen," he said, "I'm heading down to meet Thierry today. You need to get your mind off this. Why don't you come with me?"

"Clive's coming to see me in four hours. Four fucking hours, Sebby. This is no joke. What the hell am I going to tell him? I haven't got my end."

"I want you to duck him for a few days."

"Right," I said. "I'll leave him an IOU. You think he'll mind?"

"I'm being serious. You need to trust me on this. The best way to convince them you're on the up and up is to make them believe you've got a problem with money. You saw how happy Keegan was when you churned the win on Kilkelly. This may be in the opposite direction, but it's still the same thing."

And here I blundered rudely into the bleakest fact of my situation: I had to go on Sebby's word, because Sebby's was the only word I had coming to me. It was another one of those things I hadn't thought through carefully ahead of time, because I'd been too busy thinking about the money we'd make.

We met Thierry an hour south, at a chrome-and-glass diner just off the turnpike. The other customers were all exhausted wiseguys or ghosted Atlantic City hustlers, and the dining room reverberated with accounts of the long night, the boosted goods humped, and the pat hands lost. Sebby and I ordered lunch, and Thierry asked the Czech waitress, who had six silver piercings in her left ear, for black coffee and ice water. Thierry had assumed the pale, slightly wasted look of a jockey who is consistently making weight. By now I knew how to spot that look, even from a distance. His teeth were white, so I assumed he had them bonded.

"How does your wife feel about the weight?" I asked.

"She worries," he said. "Although she worries more about a spinal."

"I would, too," Sebby said. "If that happened to me—"

Sebby pantomimed firing a gun into his temple.

"They've got a trust that looks out for the jockeys who come up paralyzed," Thierry said. "Someone started a collection. It doesn't much help, though. A lot of riders check out after that happens. Sometimes they've got to hire someone to help them do it."

He crossed himself.

"You know anyone that's happened to?" Sebby asked.

"Sure," Thierry said. "Mostly they get it in the steeplechase, so I stay away from the steeplechase. The horses take one look at the pit, decide they can't make it, and stop dead.

You flip over the bridle right onto the back of your neck, and your spine turns into a bag of marbles."

"What would you do?" I asked. "If you had a fall like that?"

"I've got a loaded Sig Sauer in my bedside table," he said.

"He wouldn't even know how to flip off the safety," Sebby teased. "You'd just part your hair with it, Thierry."

"With a P228," he said, "it doesn't much matter where you put the bullet. The Sig's sure as shit going to get the job done."

He blew on his coffee but didn't seem interested in it.

"I'll tell you," he said, "it's no wonder some jockeys roll over, what with everything we've got to deal with."

"Things are tough all over," Sebby said.

"Right," I said, "we're all up against it."

I was finding it hard not to be sarcastic.

"Mike's getting nervous," Sebby said.

"Should I be worried?" Thierry asked.

"Not if you know how to lose," I said.

"You want a plate, Thierry?" Sebby asked. "Something small?"

Thierry shook his head. I knew it was killing him, watching us eat while he starved over a cup of black coffee he couldn't bring himself to drink, but I had very little sympathy for him at the time. The only person I sympathized with was myself.

"Why do you bother, Thierry?" I asked.

"My father was a jockey," he said.

He said this with exactly the same pride he'd used the first time, and I could see that he really meant it. It was in his bones.

"Sure," I said, "that's just great. Your father was a jockey. How utterly moving. But the races are fixed, Thierry. So you saying your father was a jockey doesn't make much sense to me. See, while you're trotting around the track, I'm the one getting calls from some psychopath who wants to dance on my head. So just make sure when the time comes you're not feeling too overwhelmed with pride about wearing your silks."

For a moment I worried he'd go for me. Instead he left the table, and in that instant I didn't care if I ever saw him again.

"Where the hell did that come from?" Sebby asked.

"I want to understand what he's up to. I want to know what he's thinking when the bell rings. If he's thinking, 'My father was a jockey,' he might not be holding the horse back the way he needs to. You understand?"

"All right," Sebby said, "but you didn't have to let him have it like that. If he's mad at us, he's sure as hell not going to ride the horse the way he should."

"Fine," I said. "It's just that it makes me want to throw up when he starts in with that 'my father was a jockey' horseshit."

Sebby looked at me like he didn't know me.

"Now I've got to go find him, Mike," he said.

Sebby went after Thierry and left me alone at the table to

watch my food turn cold. Oh, I'd had it with them, with
Sebby and Thierry. Sebby was lucky, how lucky he was, that
I owed him.

He must have found Thierry and smoothed things over,
because when he came back in he was all smiles and said he'd
pick up the check.

"I talked him down," he said. "But you've got to keep
your head. We're almost there."

"That's why I'm so nervous."

"It's all scripted. You don't have to be nervous about
anything."

He waved for the check.

"Thierry wants to bring another jockey in," he said.

"No one else, Sebby."

"He says it's the only way to guarantee it. He's got someone he says we can trust absolutely."

"No one else. It's the three of us, or we don't do it."

"Think about it. He knows the horses better than us."

I stared at the bacon grease on my plate. We all needed
each other, Thierry, Sebby, and me, but they needed me in a
very different way than I needed them. The arrangement was
delicate that way. Having three was much harder than having
two, because sometimes, when there were three of you, the
other two had designs that you didn't.

The strangest thought occurred to me. Sebby and
Thierry wanted me to have credibility. I wondered if they
were willing to let me get roughed up a little to earn it.

9

The next day I went to the bank to apply for a loan. Four other hopefuls were queued up ahead of me, so I took a seat and paged through foxed copies of last week's slicks. "Young Starlet's Heroic Fight Against Addiction—To Pornography." "Aging Rake's Lost Weekend—With Another Man?" A special piece on harmonic tremors in the northern Pacific plate: "Antediluvian Los Angeles."

After an hour of this I was invited into the back. The bank officer asked for my Social Security number and tapped out the digits with his right hand as he squinted at the screen. When my information appeared he seemed to panic.

"I see you defaulted on a credit card last year," he said.

"It was a misunderstanding," I explained.

"Of course. Have you any collateral, something to balance the loan?"

"No. Yes. I have my car."

"What make and model?"

I told him.

"Yes," he said, tapping his teeth with a pencil. "It's going to be difficult. You see, the credit report has some flags."

"How many?"

"Debt consolidation can be tricky."

"How bad is it?"

"One to ten," he said, "I'd have to give you a two."

He apologized and said that they couldn't help unless I had collateral equal to the amount of the loan. It was all very embarrassing for both of us, and I felt terrible that he'd had to say no.

That afternoon I walked uptown along Ninth Avenue to Central Park, then crossed the Great Lawn to the Met, where I sat on the steps outside the museum and watched the artists sell their paintings. Some of the paintings were very good. Whenever I studied the good paintings, I became conscious of the difference between the painters who'd made it inside the museum and those who hadn't. That's because you need luck, I thought. You need talent, but you also need luck. Luck has as much to do with it as the other thing.

With no money to spend, I began taking longs walks every afternoon, and most days ended the walk at the Met. On the days when I didn't feel guilty about walking past the guards without paying admission, I'd go inside and up the wide marble steps to the second floor, where I could look at the Goya and Velázquez collections for hours. If I studied each painting closely, I could pass hours without thinking about how hungry I was, not thinking of the bowl of rice I'd had for lunch, or the vendor outside selling almonds roasted in sugar and honey, the nuts cooked in a sloped iron bowl like a small wok, and how, while I was sitting there on the museum steps, the wind would sometimes blow the smoke from his pan over toward me, and my jaw would begin to tremble from how good it smelled. That was when the hunger was the worst, in the afternoon after I'd skipped breakfast and had eaten just a bowl of rice for lunch. I looked with envy at the corporate types I passed. Sleek tans earned on foreign shores. Clean suits and silver cell phones. Six figures and a company card. I'd never be hungry again. But no, that wasn't quite right. I'd be just as hungry as always but hungry in a different way. It was better to walk, and to hide inside with the paintings, where there were no vendors selling anything I could eat. It was better to think about how Goya was able to do so much with just a single frame, while I was still having a hard time doing much with twenty-four frames every second. I wondered if Goya had ever been hungry. Probably not. Court painter. What Goya had was like the opposite of hunger. He had far too much to digest already. He had Joseph Bonaparte, *Los Desastres de la Guerra,* exile, and deafness. That would have been enough for four lifetimes. It was no wonder he'd started painting the canvas black.

I made the unforgivable mistake one afternoon of passing a bakery. The bakers were lining the display case with the evening's breads, sandwiches, and pastries. There were pissaladière, and croques messieurs, and grilled crostini painted with olive oil and fresh herbs. "I'd have that one, first," I said to myself. "I'd have them heat it up, and I'd eat it standing here on the sidewalk. Then I'd get two of the rolls and take them home, where I'd crack them and bake them with ham and gruyere. A glass of Givry would be good with that." I started thinking about all the other things I'd have, listing them in my mind. Then I noticed that people were looking at me strangely in the glass, some of them grinning with amusement, and I realized I'd been talking to myself.

With wicked resolve, I walked five blocks south to a pawnshop I'd passed the day before and sold my watch for a third of what it was worth. Then I walked back to the bakery, bought the grilled bread I'd been looking at, and ate the entire thing there on the bench outside, with the crumbs falling onto my shirt and the lovely grease painting my fingers. Everyone was still looking at me, even the bakers, but I didn't care. My hands were shaking as I ate. I didn't think I'd ever tasted anything so good. I spent most of what was left from the pawnshop on the rolls and some ham and gruyere and a bottle of Givry, but of course soon after I'd finished all that, with hours to go before bed, I was hungry again, and nothing had been solved.

It came back at you and then came back at you again. I was that much angrier with my old man for having been right again. "What you want isn't for sale," he'd said, and he'd been right. You never got enough of the things you wanted. You only got a little taste, and you were that much hungrier in the end for having got it.

Near dawn I had a dream that Los Angeles was burning. It was deep night in the dream and my mother and I were up in the hills, high up on Mulholland Drive, where we could see fires for miles, and, as if moving through deep water, she pointed to the hill behind me, where the Hollywood sign was burning, and she said, I told you to be careful, Michael. Now look what you've done. The dream dissolved as I was trying to explain that I'd just made a mistake, that I hadn't meant to burn it down. Someone was lightly holding my foot. For a confusing moment I thought that I was at home and my father had awakened me to say good-bye before work.

I experienced a sudden thud of panic when I saw that it was Clive who'd awakened me. He looked tired and strung out, pale as winter light, and he seemed to have been awake all night on speed or adrenaline or both. The corners of his eyes wrinkled as he smiled at me. Two others, shorter than Clive but every bit as solidly built, waited in the living room. They looked just as strung out. I guessed he'd given them a

night out on the town in exchange for this, what they were
going to do with me.

"You have any coffee, Mike?" Clive asked.

I said I did.

"Why don't you get yourself dressed and make me some?"

Clive sat on the couch and smoked a cigarette. The other
two had sat on the windowsills. I reheated yesterday's coffee,
cutting the bitterness with plenty of milk and sugar, and
brought him a cup. Clive closed his eyes with the first sip and
lay his head back on the couch.

"Thank God," he said.

I sat at the table.

"I was out of town," I explained.

One of the two he'd brought along laughed.

Without raising his head, Clive said, "Early morning. I
saw a doc on the TV says the DEA does all their busts early
in the morning. TV logic. That's where I learned it. Once
they've got all the evidence they need, they show up at his
doorstep at five A.M. and lay on the buzzer. Dimwit comes to
the door in his underwear. Boof. He's in zip cuffs before he
knows what's happened. Not a shot fired. Early morning. I
figure, good enough for the DEA, good enough for me."

He lifted his head and looked at me.

"You weren't out of town," he said. "I can tell just by
looking at you. You were here, but you were ducking me, because you don't have it."

"Yes," I said.

"That makes a mess of things."

I said I guessed it did.

"What should we do about this, Mike?" Clive asked.

"I've got half."

"But I need all of it. Because half is half, Mike. You understand? All is all, and half is half."

"I can get all of it. I just need a couple of days."

"You've had a couple of days. Maybe you need some encouragement. Maybe we should take you down to the kennel. They have rottweilers there they feed nothing but gunpowder and ground glass. Or maybe we should take you for a swim in the East River. What do you think about that?"

How, I wondered, did we arrive at this, Clive? Where did you come from? What fathered you? It was there in his eyes. He liked it. Violence helped him make sense of it all. There was something in him that couldn't be resolved, and had to come out this way.

Clive stood up, carefully set his cigarette on the edge of the side table, and then crossed the room to me.

"Get up for a second, will you?" he asked.

"Listen," I said, "there's no need."

I was on my hands and knees on the carpet. Clive had punched me hard in the face. It was the first time I'd been punched in the face since the eighth grade. I could feel a small chip of tooth on my tongue. I spat and was surprised to see that my saliva was bright red on the wood floor. The sight of my blood brought the panic boiling up.

"Wait a minute," I said. "Wait a minute, gents. We can work this out—"

I felt if I could just explain, he would stop.

Clive pulled my wrists behind my back and bound them with plastic zip cuffs. The two others were in the kitchen now, going through the cabinets.

"Wait a minute," I said. "We just need to fix things up—"

"Under the sink," Clive said.

He lifted me up and sat me on the chair, then pulled out another chair and sat across from me.

"This is the second time you're sending me home without what I was sent for, Mike," Clive said. "It makes me look bad. Very bad. Can you understand that? It makes me look like I'm someone Keegan can't depend on."

I told him I was sorry about that, and I really was. I was sorry that we were all alone in this. In a weird way I sympathized with him, in the same way I'd sympathized with the bank manager.

"If Keegan thinks he can't get what he needs from me," Clive said, "he's going to get someone else to manage his book, and then I'll be out on the street. My wife won't have a man for a husband. My kids will starve. Can you understand why that might bother me? Can you understand why that might get me upset, driving up and down the coast after you and your lousy fiver kite?"

I nodded.

"Good," he said. "Now, the problem is, I can't go home empty-handed a third time. The Irish are superstitious, see, and three is just about the most unlucky number in the world, except for seven."

"And eleven," one of the others said from behind me.

"Right," Clive said. "And eleven. And Keegan's no exception. He sees bad things in threes. Very bad things. You do three on a match in his bar, he'll eighty-six you for life. I've seen him do it."

"Or a hat on a bed," the other one said behind me.

"I understand," I said. "Really."

"You say you do. But I've got to believe that you do. It's important that you understand just how serious I am."

I was about to answer when a clear plastic bag came down over my head. It was the bag I'd carried the rolls home in yesterday. At first I didn't realize what was happening. Then I understood. One of them held the bag, and the second one held me. Clive retrieved his cigarette and sat across from me, smoking as they held me. It must have gone on at least a minute. It was like trying to eat my own throat.

When they took the bag away I sucked in air, and felt every hungry cell in my body cry out for more. My vision was sparkling.

"Please," I said. "We can work this out."

"Tell me something, Jacobs," Clive said. "Did you think we wouldn't come find you? Did you think we'd just forgot about you?"

"I was hoping—" I said, and sucked in another lungful of air, "that Keegan had extended my debt."

"You had hoped?" he asked. "Did you think God would reach right down and fix the books Himself?"

"No," I said.

"I'll bet you did. I don't know a single loser like you who doesn't pray for His help. Help me this one time, Jesus. Give me this last win, Christ. You sure you don't look to Him?"

"Yes," I said.

"Why not?"

I wasn't exactly sure. It had something to do with the fact that He had created these three men, and then had given them the means to suffocate and beat me. There seemed to be no end to His mistakes.

"I guess I don't trust Him," I said. "Aren't you afraid of Him?"

He punched me hard in the face, so hard my head rocked back, and then nodded to the others. They put the bag over my head again. It made it so much worse to struggle, but you couldn't help struggling. Clive sat watching me, smoking ruminatively, until they took the bag away. I slid bonelessly off the chair onto my back, and they left me on the floor. Fireflies looped and pinwheeled at the edge of my vision. My lips had gone numb.

Clive knelt down over me. He stabbed his cigarette out on the wood floor and asked, "Are you convinced, Mike? Have I made it absolutely clear that I don't want to come back empty-handed a third time?"

"Yes," I said. "Yes."

"I don't need to put the bag over your head again?"

"No," I said. Pink tears dripped from my chin. "Not again."

He exhaled the last of the smoke through his nose, and the corners of his eyes wrinkled again as he smiled at me. His irises were dark, almost black, tipped with green at the edges. The tattoo on the inside of his left wrist said, "Diabetic."

"You understand everything?" he asked.

I did. Being suffocated had made it all very clear. The logic had arrived in the form of a weirdly obvious syllogism:

A smart man would pay Clive the money he owes.

I am a smart man; I owe Clive money.

I will pay Clive the money I owe.

"Yes," I said. "Yes."

Clive reached behind his back and brought out a pistol, an old revolver with duct tape on the stock. He cocked it and pointed it at my face, and my bowels seemed to turn to water.

I could see the whirled rifling inside the barrel. My entire world seemed to collapse into it.

"Open up, Mike," he said.

I did as I was told. He placed the barrel of the pistol in my mouth. It tasted oily and metallic. I gagged against the pressure on my tongue and feared for a moment I'd mess myself, like a child.

"You duck me again," he said, "you get this. Got it?"

I nodded. I understood now.

"Good," he said.

He took the pistol back and holstered it again, and the three of them left without another word. I listened as their voices dissolved into the silence of the stairwell, watching the dust motes catch fire as they passed through a bar of morning sunlight, and thinking with the false clarity that follows pain.

10

spent the last few dollars from the pawnshop buying gauze, tape, and the strongest painkillers I could find, the sort that prophesied death or coma or at any rate liver damage for the careless consumer. As I waited in the drugstore line, I swallowed four. They hit me outside the Portuguese restaurant on Spring Street, and seemed to knock the world off its axis. I sat on a bench to wait for the vertigo to pass. The bartender came outside and explained that I was scaring the diners. I asked him for a drink of water. He said I'd have to go or he'd call the police.

I had fished my keys from my pocket, and was considering and reconsidering financial options to prevent a third visit from Clive, when I noticed Father DiBenedetto sitting on the steps in front of my building. As I said his name, he stood up and came to me with a package under one arm.

"Mike," he said, "what happened to you?"

I didn't answer for a moment. The vertigo had come over me again, accompanied this time by a viselike migraine, and for a few awful seconds I feared that I was going to be sick.

"Help me upstairs, will you?" I asked.

He took my bag, and placed a hand against my back as we went up the steps into the dark foyer.

"What happened to you?" he asked again.

He had the same tight-lipped expression as the bank manager.

He helped me up to my apartment, led me over to the couch, and drew a glass of water from the tap for me. Even drinking water brought the vertigo back, so I lay back on the couch and asked him to pull the drapes.

"What else can I do, Mike?" he asked.

"Nothing at all. It's really nothing, Father."

Father DiBenedetto had been around. Before he'd gone to the seminary he'd been a longshoreman and had probably seen this sort of thing before. I wondered if it was about money those times, too.

"What's in the package?" I asked.

"I brought you my photos from Bombay. I thought you'd like to see them, since we talked about them the other night."

"That was kind of you. I would like to see them."

He looked about and in a telegraphed instant took in the

split zip cuffs, the garnet stains on the wood floor. It was all there.

"What happened to you, Mike?" he repeated.

"It isn't what you think."

"I don't know what to think."

"Please," I said. "I don't want to have to lie to you."

He brought the bag from the pharmacy over to the couch and butterflied my eye and lip with the speed and skill of a boxing cornerman. After he'd finished, he held my chin in his hand and looked closely at my left eye. The blood vessels had burst around the perimeter of the left iris, and a blind spot seemed to be gathering at the edge of my vision.

"How bad is it?" he asked.

"There's a blind spot off to the left. It won't go away."

"I've a parishioner who's an ophthalmologist. I'll ask if he can see you tomorrow."

"I haven't the money for it, Nick."

He didn't seem to mind me calling him by his first name.

"Funny," he said, "I'd always had the impression your family was wealthy."

He extracted a promise that I'd call and drew me another glass of water from the tap before he left.

Every few minutes the reeling vertigo surged over me, space uncoiling like the line spooling from my father's fishing tackle, and I'd have to close my eyes and wait for it to go away. As I lay there, I was very conscious of my mother's needlepoint on the wall. She liked to remind me that temptation was all around us, and said that God sometimes sent His angels to us in terrifying disguises to thwart that temptation. He did this, she said, because He loved us, and He wanted us to be right with Him, whatever the cost.

I sat up carefully, and when the vertigo didn't come, I crossed the room to the phone and dialed Beck's cell phone. The migraine had receded, but the blind spot was still there, off to the left. It was in the shape of a man sitting in a chair. He seemed to be watching me, but each time I looked at him he slipped away, always just out of my line of vision.

Beck answered on the first ring.

"Where are you?" I asked.

"Copenhagen," she said. "Music in Tivoli. How have you been?"

"I've been all right," I said.

"You won't forget to pick me up?"

She'd asked me to give her a ride back from Kennedy next week.

"I need to borrow some money," I said.

She drew in a breath. I sat there picturing her hands, and waited.

"I knew it," she said. "Mike, I knew it. I knew you'd call. You don't need Jay. You can make the film on your own, and it'll be great. You don't need Jay at all."

"No," I said, "I guess I don't."

Father DiBenedetto's photographs had begun to fade. Here was Nicholas DiBenedetto, at least twenty-five years younger, in beard and starched collar, surrounded by a covey of smiling children, their teeth as white as piano keys. Here was grinning young Nicholas DiBenedetto squatting at the edge of the Jumna River. Astride a royal cenotaph, with special walking staff and wrapped white scarf. In the wheat market at Panipat, swatting flies. He hadn't distanced himself from any of it. Quite the opposite. Squalor all around him, and yet always grinning, as if he really had developed a new way of seeing.

Beck's assistant messengered me a cashier's check the next morning. I wired Keegan fifty-five hundred dollars, the five thousand I'd lost plus the ten-point vigorish, the fee you were charged whether you'd won or lost. Like getting shot and then being charged for the bullet. How well Clive had motivated me—how he'd raised me, with his gun and his brute style, to the inspired state of fear. Just as fear could prevent you from doing things, it could also help you do things you'd never thought you were capable of: steal from a friend, for example. And lie. If we didn't manage to make things work with Thierry, Beck would have to hear the truth. And that would be that.

With the book settled, the calls from Clive stopped. In the

grim wake of violence, I discovered that I was furious with Sebby. This did not surprise me. Though I didn't believe he'd intended for me to get hurt, it was still his advice that I'd followed. I tried to rationalize the anger away and said to myself, "It's not his fault Clive's such a hair trigger," and, "He knows what it's like. He'd never have wanted that to happen to you," and, "If there was any design here, it was Thierry's," but of course none of it did any good. The logic was chaotic and spineless, and it couldn't withstand the simpler, more direct, more seductive voice of my temper, which reminded me that I'd suffered the worst beating of my life for taking Sebby's word at face value. The son of a bitch. He'd allowed this to happen, because he'd known all along he wasn't the one who'd get hurt. Him and that fucking jockey. I wished him a bad-luck run in the steeplechase. I wished him ten of them.

When I realized the anger wasn't going to pass, I got my blood up and dialed Sebby's number. I was too angry to hang up when his machine cut in. "Laslo," I said (because in my mind he'd already been demoted to Laslo), "I had a visit from Clive. He was more upset than you said he'd be, and now I look like a Tod Browning extra. I was able to get the money from Beck, but still. This is your doing, and next time—" Here I paused, wondering if I really wanted to go ahead with this next step, and decided that I did. "Next time this happens, the first thing out of my mouth is that I'm laying bets for you."

Because I felt bad about lying to Beck, I used the rest of the cash to buy DV tapes, but with nothing to film, I ended up walking around afternoons with the camera in its pack, my bruised eye concealed by black wraparound sunglasses. I didn't take a single frame of film. The cuts on my face had begun to heal, but five days later the black eye was worse, the colors spreading and lightening to sunrise yellows, and I'd begun to suffer nightly migraines. The blind spot had grown and intensified, always and forever there at the left edge of my vision, giving me the unpleasant sensation of being watched. I spent a lot of time wondering if I'd done the right thing, leaving that message for Sebby. It seemed improvident to offer threats. He hadn't called, which meant he was out of town and hadn't got the message.

And what's he up to? I wondered. Honestly—where do you think he goes when he vanishes? Not always to visit his father. Is it really so impossible to think he's exercising that monkey on his back elsewhere? Because when he doesn't go in for horses, he goes in for cards. And when he doesn't go in for cards, he goes in for horses. He's the kind of guy who thinks he can win at three-card monty.

After five afternoons of dud hikes with the camera, I gave up and visited the nearest octoplex, where I took in the only film running for the next hour, the latest Hollywood bloodbath. It was a three-hour, billion-dollar snuff flick, the sort where the villains identify themselves by their bad oral hygiene, and rather than transport or anesthetize me, it merely filled me with a deep sense of despair. This was the end of the path I'd picked. One hundred years from the Lumières to this.

I fled the theater long before the last villain had been beheaded or blown up or sucked into a vortex, bought a newspaper, and took a seat at the bar at the Blind Tiger. The bartender seemed not to notice my face. It was Beck's money I was spending, so I sat and thought about her hands and read the paper. The news seemed very removed from me. The assassination of yet another theocrat. Oil wells burning in distant deserts. A color photograph beneath the strapline, four columns wide: the sky a burning biosphere of black smoke. Marines were dying every day, kids who'd been killed by other kids toting satchel bombs. Death, I reflected, was good at what it did. Death narrowed things down nicely. That's a lovely way of looking at things. You really are in a funk.

I lingered until long past dark. Even alcohol couldn't cut through the funk that had overtaken me. It got me good and drunk, though, without any food, and I hoped I was drunk enough that I'd be able to sleep without any dreams.

Those steep steps of home—the stairwell, with its smell of dejection. Thirty-nine steps, just like the film: that was why I'd rented the place. I unlocked my door, and had just dropped the keys in the glass bowl when my father sat up on the couch, rubbing his eyes and saying my name.

11

He crossed the room and gave me a hug that hurt every-where. The hug enveloped me in a familiar smell of pipe tobacco, mint, and steel shavings, and I didn't think I'd ever been so acutely aware of who this man was and what he meant to me. I was happy to see him and terribly embarrassed for him to see me this way. He was standing a foot away from me, two inches shorter yet commanding much more of a presence, with his hands grasping my elbows. He looked closely at my black eye, at the healing cuts that framed it.

"Mike," he said, "my God, what's happened to you?"

"It's nothing. Look. See? It's not that bad."

He held my chin in his fist, as Father DiBenedetto had, and turned my face back and forth in the lamplight.

"Not that bad?" he asked. "Not that bad?"

There was a look on his face I'd never seen before, a

guarded worry that threatened to unravel into hysteria, and in a sick way it gave me a lot of satisfaction. For once he wasn't the wisest guy in the room, and he didn't know what to do about it.

"Mike," he said, "what did they do to you?"

I didn't answer. He sat on the couch and I sat at the kitchen table and we waited there in silence for a moment. You'd think I'd just told him I had cancer, the look he had. I couldn't imagine how it was for a father to see his son that way, but I guessed it wasn't too pleasant. He kept picking up his hat and putting it down. I'd always thought that he wore the hat as an affectation, a reference to his slightly dated orientation, but I understood now that it was more of a prop that gave him something to do with his hands when he was under stress. He had more money than almost anyone I knew and could lay off twenty men without losing sleep, but the sight of me like this was enough to make him go to pieces. It's funny the places where people are fragile.

"I fell down the stairs," I said. "Really, Dad. I slipped and fell. That's all."

"That's a damned lie," he said. "You didn't slip. Father Nicholas called me."

"I wish he hadn't."

"He said somebody had roughed you up."

"It was just a bar fight," I said.

He was turning his hat over in his hand.

"I couldn't sleep at night," he said, "if I thought some-thing was wrong."

"Nothing's wrong, Dad. Not anymore."

"Promise me."

I promised him. He set his hat beside him and rubbed his eyes. Though he was in very good shape and his hair still had much of its color, he looked very old, and I realized I was largely responsible for that. He hadn't ever stopped being my father, even after I'd moved out, and I'd been just as difficult as an adult as I had been as a kid.

"How long have you been here?" I asked.

"All day," he said. "I went to see your movie."

I'd always hated it when he called my films "movies."

"I thought the run had ended," I said.

"I guess not."

"What did you think?" I asked.

"Mike, it was so good. It was terrific. It was the best movie you've made."

When you've known someone well for a long time and have accustomed yourself to his tics and habits, you come to know very easily when he's lying to you. In past years I had watched a great many friends and family lie to me and tell me, with forced sincerity, how much they had enjoyed my latest film. It was obvious enough that the moment I left the room they were going to roll their eyes and ask each other in low voices why in the world someone would see a "movie" like that. It didn't bother me that they didn't like my films—most of them thought *The Sound of Music* was as good as film could get—but their lies enraged me. There was absolutely none of that falseness in my father's manner now, and I was a little bit shocked to see that he'd been moved almost to the point of tears by the film. You could see it in his face.

"I, ah, I hadn't—I didn't think you'd like it so much," I said.

"No, no," he said. "It was incredible, Mike. Having the patients work the camera? It was fascinating, the way you strung all the stories together and made them play off each other. It made me understand what it was like for them."

"When did you get here?" I asked.

"I took the day off. Got here after lunch and waited for a few hours. I hope you don't mind that I let myself in. After I'd waited for a while I called Father Nicholas, and he told me where I could see your movie. I had some trouble finding the place, but eventually I got myself there. I got back about an hour ago. Bought you some bourbon."

It was there on the kitchen counter. As it was one of those rare occasions that he was away from my mother's deeply entrenched disapproval of liquor, he'd finished about a fifth of the bottle, but as usual you would never know that he'd had even a single drink.

"Have you eaten?" I asked.

"No," he said. "I was waiting for you. By the way, your

friend called. Sebby. He asked me to tell you he was sorry about Clive."

I said that was good to hear.

"Let's bring him to dinner," he said. "You think he's free?"

We walked up the street to Pastis. As we were being shown to an outside table I heard Sebby call my name. He came through the bar crowd with a grim expression on his face, and for the first time that I could recall he gave me a hug. He had the same look my father had worn when he first saw my face. All the anger went out of me. Anyone could see that he hadn't meant for anything to happen.

As soon as they sat down, Sebby and my father began talking about me as if I wasn't there at the table with them, discussing how polished *The Daisy Chain* had been, what a great "movie" it was, and what a curiosity it was that not many people had gone to see it. What a curiosity, indeed. They had always got along well, Sebby and my father.

"What's next, Mike?" my father asked.

"Mike's next film is going to blow everyone away," Sebby said.

He glanced at me with a sly expression I knew well. It was the look he wore whenever he was trying to work an angle.

Not this, I thought. Not this, Sebby. Anything but this.

"It couldn't be better than this one," my father said. "Impossible. Impossible."

He was exultant with drink and pride.

"Absolutely," Sebby said. "This next one's going to put him on the map."

"What's it about?" he asked.

"Horse racing," I said quietly.

"I love the horses," my father said. "Have you ever been to the track? Beautiful animals? Ah! Such beauty in the way they run. They run like they don't even know people are watching. Do it just for the joy of it. We should all be so lucky, to not even know that people are betting on us. It's a shame they bet on them. It makes it all seem so—"

"Dishonest," I said. "Corrupt."

"Exactly," Sebby agreed. "It's the dishonesty that Mike's really digging into. It's going to be a great film."

"Have you started?" my father asked.

"Not yet," Sebby said, still looking at me sideways. "See, we haven't got the financing. Mike's doing this one all on his own. He's decided he doesn't need a production company. He doesn't like it when producers interfere with his vision."

I thought my father was going to come up out of his chair. He slapped his hat against his leg with happiness and called inside the dining room to the waitress to bring a bottle of champagne. She gave him the same look the waiters there are always giving people from out of town.

"You don't need to do that, Dad," I said.

I was sick about the whole thing, about what I was doing

with him, and with Beck. He'd been worried about me and had come to check up on me, and here we were, taking him, the same way I'd taken her.

"Don't look so glum, Mike," my father said. "You made a great, great movie."

"They're films, Dad," I said.

I regretted saying it as soon as I saw the look on his face.

"I'm sorry," he said softly. "Sometimes I don't know the right words. I just wanted you to know how proud I was of you."

The waitress brought the champagne.

"My son made a great film," my father explained.

There were tears in his eyes.

"That's nice," she said in a bored voice.

After she had poured the champagne, Sebby asked, "What should we drink to, Henry?"

We looked around at each other.

"I'll say something," my father said. "I'd like to, if it's all right with Mike."

For a moment I thought he was going to get to his feet. He had this embarrassed look on his face that I'd seen only once before, on the day I'd graduated from film school, but that day he hadn't said anything and I'd never quite known what he was thinking. There was no question what he was thinking now. He was looking right at me, happy and drunk on bourbon and pride. I was embarrassed for him, because I could see that he was about to be completely honest with me. It was going to infuriate me, what he was about to say, because I'd made him right by making such a good film, and because he still had no sense of what it had cost me to get it made. I was grateful and furious with him at the same time.

"Mike," he said, "it's important to me that you understand what you've done. There were times when I doubted your move to New York, even though I have always forcefully encouraged you to pursue what you loved. I now see that I was wrong to ever doubt you. I make objects out of steel for the government. What makes me successful is that I can make each object exactly the same way, down to the micrometer, so that no two objects are ever dissimilar. God Himself couldn't tell one from the other, which means I'm successful because I'm invisible. The opposite is true of you. You've made something that will never be duplicated. No matter what happens, even if you never make another, ah, *film,* you will always have made this one. This great one. No one can ever take that away from you. Which means that no one can ever take that from me, either."

"Excuse me," I said.

Pastis has European-style bathrooms, with water closets and a big communal sink room for men and women. Both water closets were taken, so I had to stand there in the middle of the sink room and let the tears go. Everyone at the sinks was embarrassed for me, just as I'd been embarrassed for my father a moment ago, and with my hideous black eyes and my tears and my split lip, I could only imagine what they thought of me. That was the worst of it, the thought that they pitied me, because after a certain point you're responsible for who and what you are and don't deserve people's sympathy. I was going to lie to him to take his money. I was going to use his trust against him, the way I had with Beck, which is the worst thing anyone can do to someone else.

When I had stifled the tears, I put cold water on my face. The tears, I reasoned, were useless. It was already decided, and now there was only the doing. I already knew how I felt about it, but I was going to do it anyway.

My father stopped into the bathroom on our way out. Sebby and I waited on the sidewalk.

"I'm sorry about Clive, old man," he said.

"It doesn't hurt as much anymore. I get migraines, though. Every fucking night!"

"You're all right with this?" he asked.

"No," I said, "I don't think I'll be all right ever again."

My father and I walked home in silence. We were drunk and full, and I sensed that the silence was very comfortable for him. I said I'd take the couch and made up the bed for him. He turned in right away, and in a few minutes I heard him breathing quietly from the next room.

It was a long time before I slept. I woke later in the dark. There had been a sound out on the fire escape. I went to the window and threw it open. My father came into the living room in his boxer shorts.

"What was it?" he asked.

"I think it was a bat. They get up under the eaves."

He hesitated.

"You're sure I don't need to worry?" he asked.

"You'd know," I said. "I wouldn't be able to hide it."

"All right," he said. "Is five thousand good to start?"

"It's plenty," I said.

I could hardly bring myself to say it.

"Fine," he said. "Good night, Mike."

"Good night, Dad."

When I woke in the morning, he was gone. A check for five thousand dollars was taped to the hall mirror. I cashed it, then walked home and cried in the bathroom, with my mother's needlepoint watching me from the wall.

12

I am very much worrying at seeing you like this," Popoloskouros said. "To get such a face you have to first be causing people a lot of trouble. I am wondering if you are here to be causing me a lot of trouble."

It was Sebby's idea that I visit Popoloskouros while my bruised eye was still a blighted palette of decaying reds and blues. The worse I looked, he figured, the more legitimate I'd seem, which meant I must have looked plenty legitimate.

"It was a misunderstanding," I said.

"Of course," he said. "Everything is a matter of miscommunication with a degenerate. He will steal the food off your plate and tell you he was merely doing the dishes."

I could see that he was convinced.

"Have you had any luck?" he asked.

"I had a big win with someone named Keegan, down at

the shore. Five to one on a five-hundred lay at Aqueduct. A filly named Kilkelly."

Popoloskouros nodded.

"He is having a nice bar down in Cape May," he said. "And so. It was his boy Clive who did this to you."

I didn't answer.

"I am not liking Clive very much," Popoloskouros said. "Every other word is fuck this and fuck that and then fucking the other thing. The man has no dignity. I would not trusting him around my daughters."

I sipped the glass of retsina he'd poured for me and winced.

"That's why I came to see you," I said.

"Keegan is no longer being trusted?"

"I trust Keegan. But I dislike Clive as much as you."

Popoloskouros nodded.

"I am thinking Clive is a problem for people like me," he said. "Everyone except him is thinking the violence is something you are doing when you have no other choice. He is using it first and last and always, and without thinking ahead of the problems that come. Eventually he is going to rough up the son of a senator or a police captain. And then the state attorney general is opening a grand jury, and we all are having a lot of problems."

"I'd think you'd always have problems with the police."

"Only in the fall, when the American football games

come around. All the big bookmakers get their money from the football games. That's why I stick with the horses. I am having very little trouble with them."

That was good, that he disliked Clive. It would make him want my bets, to pull business away from Keegan, and from Clive. After I had convinced Popoloskouros, I was going to visit the eight other bookmakers Sebby and Thierry knew, open a line with each of them, and then visit Keegan and ask if I could reopen my book with him. I'd tell him I understood now, that the mistake had been mine. He'd grin his superstitious Irish grin and pat my hand and tell me that he was sorry things had worked out that way. It made me feel good, knowing I was going to clean his wallet, and knowing I'd never have to see his lying Irish face again. If I ever got him alone I'd tattoo the number three right on his forehead.

Tomorrow I would place a bet of two thousand dollars with each of the ten bookmakers on a sure loser. Any questions about my legitimacy, Thierry said, would be resolved when the new bookmakers asked around and heard what Clive had done to me. A final loss would erase any lingering doubts. This Saturday I would call each of them again to place another bet, this time for one thousand dollars, on a quinella for the sixth race at Aqueduct. If anyone wasn't willing to give me a line of three thousand total, I would roll that share of the money to another bookmaker. Thierry said he'd found another jockey to join us, someone named Vato who was running with him in the sixth race, with a clear field of three for win, place, and show, with Thierry on the sure bet and Vato on the placer.

"I talked to Sebby about this," I said. "I made it clear. I don't want anyone else. It's bad enough with three."

"It's a one-time thing. We pay him, and it's like it never happened."

"You seem awfully sure."

"This kid," Thierry said, "he's silent as the grave."

Maybe, I thought, that's not such a great way of putting it.

"I understand," Thierry said quietly. "You're worried. But you've got to trust me on this. It has to be this way. I can't make it happen alone."

They would run together, he said, blocking any lanes by squaring the front of the pack, until they reached the quarter pole, where Thierry would push anyone threatening the quinella into the post. It was as foolproof as any fixed horse race could be, and he was absolutely sure this was our heat.

I'd always thought of Sebby as running the betting, but now, with the race so close, I could see it was all Thierry. He said he expected to find odds of one hundred to one, so the bets had to be spread among at least ten bookmakers. We had to lose big as soon as possible, and lose foolishly, since we were going to take such a big win at Aqueduct. Most book-makers didn't like each other, he said, and spoke to each other only when they absolutely had to lay off any bad odds, and even then only through intermediaries, so we didn't have to worry that they'd learn there were multiple bets being placed.

With such a big payoff, he added, there were bound to be some problems with the figures on the back end, but that couldn't be helped. The bookmakers didn't like to make big payoffs, and some of them wouldn't pay at all, knowing that there was nothing we could do without hiring some Camden muscle. It usually didn't come to that, since it was bad for a bookmaker's reputation not to cover a bet, especially with someone from New York, but if the payout was big enough it was worth it to hold on to it. We would just have to take it as a matter of course.

When I had finished talking with Thierry, I took the notepad off the refrigerator, sat at my desk, and wrote in pencil:

$$10,000 \times 100 =$$

I sat thinking for a moment, listening to the clock tick in the hall, and then added:

$$10,000 \times 100 = 1,000,000$$

It was a real shock to see it there before me, that cryptogram, that benchmark of wealth, with its comet's tail of zeroes. String a line of nothings together, you've got nothing and more nothing. But place a one out in front of them, in just the right place, at just the right time, and everything turns. Turns like life. You lost and lost and lost, and poured your heart out just to take a step backward, but if you played a win in the right column, at the right time, everything was different and all was forgiven.

And what was all this money going to buy us? The answer seemed simple enough. We were going to buy back all the time we'd lost in Los Angeles. Sebby's big, beautiful nightmare. All the time we'd given up because the bills said we had to. That was what money bought: it bought you time. Money was your way of buying more life. The genuinely wealthy, the Rockefellers and DuPonts and Buntings and Whitfields—I wondered if they had bought so much life back that they believed they had killed Death, killed him with all their money.

I was going to go through with it. I was going to do it, because even if things went wrong I had a way out. It meant betraying Sebby, but that couldn't be helped. I had paid my debt to him, paid him by risking blood and pain for his obsession, and if that was how things had to turn out, so be it. He was right. No one ever got rich off being wise.

I called the bookmakers the next day and placed a bet of two thousand dollars with each one on a twenty-to-one nag named Gold Coast who had strained her tendon just four weeks ago. The horse could no sooner win a race than play the xylophone.

I told Popoloskouros, "I've got a good feeling about this one."

I could hear him writing the numbers down on the other end of the phone.

"So do I," he said.

Gold Coast broke down on the backstretch and walked into last place.

Down twenty thousand dollars, having bet ten more that morning, I drove to Aqueduct to watch Thierry lose the sixth race on Saturday. Sebby had wanted to come to the track, but I'd refused him, partly because I'd thought it unwise for him to be seen with me there and partly because he'd been getting on my nerves all morning, chattering non stop about how, because of the weather, the track was going to run fast, and we were sure to get rightly fucked by some odds-against nag. It was a sunny, cold April day, with a jazz band playing in the mezzanine behind my table. I've noticed that bebop, in particular the old Art Blakey pieces my father loves, seems to set people on edge, especially people who have staked money on a horse race. I could see why the track had hired them. The music was enough to make you bet poorly.

The tote board was showing five to two on Vato's horse, Holy Writ, to win, with Thierry's horse, a big seventeen-hand thoroughbred named Mother's Gate, paying even money. I sat gripping my drink and watching the horses being led from the paddock to the staging area. Thierry had called Sebby yesterday to check that everything was set. Sebby told me Thierry was nervous about the signs. His was the sixth horse in the sixth race, and he'd wondered aloud where the third six would show itself. The bad signs had spooked us all, and I promised myself that when this was over I'd never listen to Sebby, ever again. We would be friends, but that was where everything would end. I sat overlooking the track, paced my drinking, and tried not to think about the number six.

The sixth race came out of the gate on schedule. Holy Writ and Mother's Gate took the lead early, with Thierry and Vato squaring the lanes expertly against the infield rail. I was gripping the table so hard my fingertips were white. The two of them held the line perfectly through the backstretch, Thierry doing a push-pull to dictate the pace, with no horse willing to step outside the pack and risk the wind and distance to have an open lane.

We're going to win it, I thought. It's going to happen. It's going to fucking happen.

At the quarter pole, Thierry's horse seemed to flag slightly. It was like watching a ballet dancer, a glassblower, a surgeon. Thierry was leaning over the horse's neck, talking to him gently, leading him back a step at a time, and closing off any rushes from the inside. Vato had slipped four lengths ahead of Thierry, with our place horse just one length behind, and Thierry in a clear third. The pack was so close now I could see the expression on Thierry's face, smell the tobacco-and-earth odor of the loam the pack had kicked up. He was utterly relaxed, as calm as a man rocking a new baby, still talking gently to his horse and checking his flanks to be sure no one could give a burst in the homestretch. We were going to pull it off, there it was, and I had let go of the table when Mother's Gate leaped forward in an end-run so quick the crowd in the grandstand below me came to its feet with a shout. Thierry was still talking to him, but it was no good. The horse only knew how to run. I was out of my chair. He passed the show horse with one hundred yards to go, then caught up to Vato's horse, and with fifty yards to the finish line their feet tied up and both horses went over in a tangle of limbs and nostrils and white eyes, with burst tack flying and jockeys tumbling broken on the loam. Two other horses went down as they passed, one of them flipping over the rail into the infield. She jerked to her feet and broke off in a perpendicular trail, bucking and kicking her hind legs. The rest of the field went by, but I don't think a single person saw the finish.

Someone behind me said, "Look at that poor son of a bitch."

The horse in the infield had broken her foreleg. The bone flopped like a threshing flail at the end of her leg. The sight of a hurt animal had always bothered me, even more than the sight of an injured human, and this was the worst I'd ever seen. Two trainers hopped over the infield rail and ran after her, trying to calm her by holding their arms up and calling to her, but she went leaping away from them, eyes showing white, teeth bared in fear and pain. One of the four jockeys who had fallen had got up and was leading his horse by the bridle toward the finishing line. Two others were walking around drunkenly in their filthy silks, looking down at the loose track loam as if they had misplaced their car keys there. One of them walked in a circle and then sat down again. After he had sat down, I could see he was Thierry. He had dirt on his face, with blood running from his nose and left ear.

The fourth jockey hadn't got up yet. He lay with his face in the dirt, his head turned all wrong and the swivel in his neck gone loose. It was Vato, and just by looking at him you could see what had happened. In a moment the track was full of shouting people. They all seemed to be in a terrible hurry, and I realized it was because Vato wasn't breathing. Someone had backed a truck onto the track. Three EMTs knelt beside him and put a tube down his throat, then pinned him to the backboard and placed him in the bed of the truck. By now the horse that was loose in the infield had fallen down. When the trainers reached her, one of them put his knee on her neck, and she lay there quivering in the sun while the other talked to her and stroked her nose. Another trainer came walking to them carrying a black bag. Before he did it, two others carried a screen out and set it up in front of the horse, only they put the screen at the wrong angle, and everyone around me saw what happened, including the fact that the trainer still had his knee on her neck. The horse tried to get up at the last minute, as if she knew what was about to happen and wanted to get away.

The mezzanine was hushed after that, the couples at the tables quietly comforting each other. When the band started playing again, everyone stopped talking and, in a low voice that you could still hear over the music, someone behind me said, "You pigheaded sons of bitches." The band stopped playing then and began to break down their instruments. I could see that the band leader felt badly and had only been trying to help. For a moment I thought of asking him over for a drink. Then I realized I couldn't pay for the three I'd had, nor could I pay for the self-congratulatory lunch I had planned. The bets for this race would be off, but we still owed twenty thousand for the loss on the nag four days ago, money we didn't have. I had been living on borrowed optimism all day. I had been banking on something that wasn't there.

I finished my drink and paid the bill with my credit card, then walked down to the paddock. Thierry's race had been the last of the day, and most of the jockeys had already left. The paddocks were empty except for the horses and their handlers. A jockey who had changed into street clothes came walking by me with his silks and his saddle slung over his shoulder. I recognized him as one of the two jockeys who'd been walking around the track after the fall. He was a kid with a smooth Cuban face and black hair.

"I'm sorry about the fall," I said.

"Nothing," he said. "It's Vato I feel sorry for. And the horse they put down."

I could see he didn't like to talk about it.

"Is Thierry all right?" I asked.

The kid tapped his temple with his index finger.

"His head," he said, "it's not so good right now. He said the race was fixed."

I hurried back to the paddock and asked the first handler I saw where Thierry was. The handler led me past the stables to a white building just off the track. There were three beds inside. Thierry lay in the first bed still dressed in his silks. The sheets were filthy beneath him. A nurse sat at the foot of the bed reading.

"Hi, Mike," Thierry said.

"How is he?" I asked.

"He has a concussion," the nurse said.

"I don't remember what happened, Mike," he said. "I don't remember the race. I was in the paddock just before the warm-up. Then I came to, and I was sitting on the track. It's like there never was a race."

"You got tripped up riding the number six horse."

"They tell me Vato broke his neck," he said. "Is that true?"

I said I didn't know. Thierry looked at the ceiling again. You could see that he was trying not to move, even though he wanted to get up and pace the room.

"I'm not fixing any more races, Mike," he said. "It's bad luck. The last number was me on the six horse, tripping up Vato. Now I'm the bad luck."

"Thierry—"

"I'm the number six now, Mike. See?"

He shivered and crossed himself.

"You'll be all right, Thierry," I said. "You shouldn't talk."

The nurse was watching me.

"No more races, Mike," he said. "No more fixing anything. Vato's gone and broke his poor neck. He's dead, and it's all my fault."

"It's not your fault, Thierry. You just got tripped up on the number six."

"No more races, Mike," he said. "No more fixing anything."

He turned on his side, facing away from me. His silks were filthy where he had fallen to the turf. All the dignity had been taken out of him, and for the first time he seemed small and frail to me. It was amazing how much the dignity and the nice manners did for him, and now he was nothing without them.

"You'll be all right, Thierry," I said. "You want me to drive you home?"

He didn't answer.

"Thierry?" I asked, and this time I heard the fear in my voice.

"His wife is coming," the nurse said.

She followed me outside.

"What was that he was saying about the races?" she asked.

"He's out of his head."

"He's been talking about it since he came in."

"He's talking crazy," I said. "He didn't fix anything."

"You'd better hope he stops," she said.

She stood in the doorway squinting up at the sunlight.

"Listen," I said, "you're not going to tell anyone, are you?"

"He was talking from the moment they brought him in. Everyone heard him."

"What was he saying?"

"Exactly what he was saying just now."

I asked her if anyone believed him. She shrugged.

"The head injuries talk and talk," she said. "Especially the Catholic ones. They seem to think it's bad luck they brought on themselves."

She shook her head and lit a cigarette.

"He asked for a priest," she said. "He was begging for one. But we don't have one here."

Confess all you want, Thierry, I thought. But do it the way the rest of us do. In silence.

"Poor Vato," she said.

"Is he really dead?"

"No," she said. "They got him back."

She dropped her cigarette to the ground and went back inside. I walked back to the car, where I sat for a moment thinking about poor Vato. Sebby would have heard the race on the radio. There would be a message waiting for me when I got home. "Mike," he would ask, "what are we going to do?"

What am I going to do? I thought. Think about it, Sebby. There's only one place for me to go.

13

I waited half an hour for Lesch at the downtown Cipriani, nipping at ice water and pretending not to notice the bartender's increasingly disdainful looks. When Lesch arrived he made no apology for his lateness and ordered two martinis up without asking if I wanted one. I did. Drinks were useful, he said, in that they encouraged expediency. You had to get to the point before the alcohol set in and made you either too drunk or too careless to have a meaningful conversation.

"I can only have one," I said.

"Working?" he asked.

The smug son of a bitch.

"Hardly," I said.

"I'm happy you called, Mike."

"You knew I would."

"You told me you wouldn't."

"And then you forced my hand," I said.

"Absolutely untrue."

"You rejected all my proposals."

"I rejected them," he said, "because they were beneath you. Too reductive. Why not give up and begin shooting television commercials instead? You're better than that."

"Actually," I said, "I'm not."

"I've seen what you're capable of. Why don't you go back and watch *Prodigal Son*? Remember how good that was? I'd be happy to set up a screening. You need to get back to what you were trying to accomplish in the first place, with that first film."

"Why," I asked, "does everyone always want you to get back to what you've already done? I change because I like to change. Everyone wants the film to be interesting for the audience, but no one cares if making it is interesting for the filmmaker."

Lesch gave a derisive snort.

"Cry me a fucking river, Mike," he said. "This is what you've always wanted to do. Now you're doing it. You knew this before you even began. You can't make a great film and think only about yourself. That's the whole point. The better it is, the less it's got to do with you."

"Was it interesting for Godard? Was it interesting for Eisenstein?"

"I'm sure it was interesting for Riefenstahl," Lesch said.

"Fuck off."

"Really," he said. "You could make a hell of a liberal-mandate flick. *Abortionists Land at Dawn. Attack of the Killer Apologists. Revisionist Ho!*"

"Jay," I said, "you need me more than I need you."

"Not really," he said.

I was pleased to see that he didn't seem so sure.

Of course, I thought. Of course. He's afraid, and that's why he's needling you. Lesch is as governed by fear as you are. He's hoping you won't see the forest for the trees. You always have to remember that, how afraid he is, how expensive his life is, how expensive his wife and his townhouse and his tastes are. His world costs money. Everything he takes on is a drain on the thing he loves most, and that's money. It's expensive to stay wealthy.

"How is Sebby?" Jay asked. "He hasn't shown up for work in a week."

"He's working from home."

Lesch shook his head. He seemed genuinely sad for Sebby.

"Sebby was very good in his day," he said. "Very good."

"You don't know the half of it."

"I've heard some stories about him in L.A."

"They practically ran him out on a rail. I think that's why he did so well in New York. He had to prove them wrong."

"Everyone needs his L.A. story," Lesch said.

"If he was good once, he might be good again."

"He's still good."

"Then why not keep him on?"

Jay sipped his drink.

"I did some digging around," he said. "I didn't like what I found. Did you know he owes money all over Atlantic City? Associating with some very bad people, Mike. He's been betting on the horses, and now he's in over his head. I'm afraid he's going to start stealing from me."

He's been betting on the side all along, I thought. The son of a bitch. You knew you couldn't trust him. You were just his way to get back at Popoloskouros and Keegan. He's been betting on the side, and ten to one he hasn't got his share. Ten to one he's more broke than ever, and you're left to carry this debt alone.

"Let's get another round," I said.

I looked through the glass wall at the yellow Cipriani awning, at the über couples walking by on the street. Something, I reflected, had gone terribly wrong with money. Not everyone was using it to buy time; some were using it to buy physical perfection. It was moving people into a strange realm of attractiveness so far beyond good-looking it was almost grotesque. The men were prettier than the women. The women were all silicone and faux bitch veneer. I might have been on Rodeo Drive. Hollywood wasn't finished with us. We had left, but it wasn't finished with us. It was coming after us with its money, with its dreams, with its blue pools and ice sculptures. It would find us, even if we went all the way to Hong Kong.

"Are we going to do this?" I asked.

"Are we?"

"I don't have any choice, do I?"

"It would just be for a while, Mike. A year. Until I can find someone full-time. Then we'll go back to the way it was. You're going to benefit from this, I promise. Once the decks are clear, I'll be able to back something of yours. I'll get you a nice Avid studio and a stipend. I'll even hire you a PA so you don't have to digitize anything."

"What about Sebby?"

"He'll get snapped up."

"Maybe he'll go back to L.A."

"He'll get snapped up."

"He won't, though."

It was hard to say it and know it was true. Things were over for Sebby. He was finished on both coasts. I didn't know what he was going to do for his father.

"What is it you want?" Lesch asked.

"Six months' back pay for Sebby. A five-thousand-dollar signing bonus for me."

He shook his head and looked away.

"You can have the bonus," he said, "but the pay for Sebby is out of the question."

"Why?"

"I've been carrying him for six months. He's already got the six months' pay out of me. He doesn't show up for work. His corporate card has been giving me night sweats."

"Two months."

"Mike."

"Four weeks. Four weeks, or I'm prepared to say no."

"You're not, though. You wouldn't have called me if you had any other choice."

"Jay," I said. "Be decent about this."

He grinned at me. He was enjoying this.

"All right," he said. "I'll be decent about this. Five thousand for you. Sebby gets four weeks' pay. It's four weeks more than he deserves, and I'm only doing it to start things off right between us."

We finished our drinks and shook on it. Meeting adjourned.

I followed Lesch out to the curb, asked him to make it six weeks' pay, was denied, and watched the taillights of his taxi recede north on West Broadway, thinking that even Judas had got thirty pieces of silver for his betrayal. I was just drunk enough to believe that another drink was exactly what I needed, but when I turned to go back inside the bartender gave me a look colder than the dark side of the moon. Instead I walked uptown through a light rain to the White Horse Tavern and sat at the bar staring at my cell phone. It was strange being in a gloomy place like the White Horse after having two drinks in the clean, bright white space of Cipriani. Today was Sunday and the bar was empty except for three darkly smoldering drunks working through the week's pay at the end of the bar.

There was a call I had to make and I knew I wouldn't be able to sleep until I had made it. I considered, seriously considered, getting so drunk I would not remember making it. I'd make it and then leave myself a note on the bathroom mirror that said, "You told him. Go back to bed and pull the covers over your head." What a lovely coward you are. What a gutless wonder.

Sebby answered on the first ring.

"Where the hell have you been?" he asked. "I left you five messages."

"I think we should talk, Sebby," I said.

"I'm hearing bad things, Mike. Thierry is talking. This is not good. This is not good. This really is not good."

"You have a minute?" I asked. "Because, really, we should talk."

He hardly seemed to be listening.

"You want to get a drink?" he asked. "I could use a drink."

He arrived at the White Horse ten minutes later and lay his dripping jacket over the radiator to dry. The rain was falling harder now and the inside of the glass had frosted over with humidity. He sat next to me at the bar and rubbed his eyes with his palms."

"This is not good, Mike," he said. "I was up all night making calls."

"This isn't about Thierry."

He turned and looked at me.

"What," he asked, "your dad get wise to this?"

I looked into my glass.

"Call Jay," I said. "You really need to call Jay."

"Why the hell should I call Jay?"

"Just call him, Sebby."

He was watching me steadily, his expression confused and dismayed.

"Mike," he said, "the one thing we always had was that they never got us to turn on each other. That was the one thing we had on them. Tell me that isn't what's happened."

I didn't answer.

"Listen," he said. "I need you to do something for me. I need you to tell me that isn't what's happened. I need you to tell me that."

"I can't."

"Why not, Mike?" he asked. "Why can't you just do that for me?"

"Jay hired me tonight. He's going to let you go."

"How long has this been going on?" he asked.

I didn't answer.

"Mike," he asked, "how long?"

"Since the day Popoloskouros broke your thumb. It wasn't my doing. Jay pushed me into it. He said he wouldn't back any of my films unless I took the job."

"You didn't think I'd be interested to know this?"

"I didn't think I'd have to take him up on it. If the thing with Thierry had panned out it wouldn't have been a problem. But everything's changed. Everything's changed, Sebby."

"Changed? No fucking shit, Mike."

"A friend," I said stupidly, "is someone who stabs you in the front."

"I expected this from Jay. But I never guessed you'd be the one to help him do it."

"You've been betting on the side. You know. I know. Don't act the angel. I was forced into this spot."

"Maybe," he said. "Maybe. But I never turned on you, Mike."

"Vato's neck is broken. Thierry told the nurse we fixed the race. We owe more cash than I've seen in ten years. At least this way I don't get thrown down the stairwell. You can see that, can't you? It was this or nothing."

"Anything but this," he said. "Give me anything but this."

"I wish I could. But this is all I've got. This, and four weeks' pay."

"Mike," he said, "never mind that this was my livelihood. Never mind my father, and what this means for him. Never mind that I gave you your first break. I thought we were building something together, something that would prove that people like us can succeed *despite* people like Jay. And then you cut me out of it, because it was inconvenient for you not to cut me out. They have a word for what you did. That word is betrayal."

"Clive just about killed me, Sebby. Put a fucking bag over my head and *left it there.* It's not about convenience."

"You could have got the rest from your father."

"I couldn't lie to him again," I said. "Not that."

"Ah," he said, "one's your limit, yes?"

I didn't answer. He took his change and left a tip.

"I've got to ship out," he said. "Good to see you, old man."

"You've got to forgive me, Sebby. You've got to see this from my side."

"Sure thing," he said. "You've got my blessing."

He was smiling, but his eyes were tipped with a high gloss of fury. It was the first time I'd ever been afraid of him. He got up and took his jacket from the radiator.

"I'll see you later, Mike," he said.

I followed him out, but he wouldn't look at me. I stood in the rain watching him walk away and then went back inside.

"He doesn't look too happy," the bartender said.

"Not a bit."

"What's he mad about?"

"I took his job."

The bartender, who resembled Keegan, placed an upside-down shot glass beside my beer, which I had hardly touched, and rapped his knuckles on the bar. He looked like he'd seen this sort of thing a hundred times before.

"On me, babe," he said.

"It wasn't how I wanted things to turn out."

" 'Course not."

It was important to me that he understand.

"Anyway," he said, "the walk's probably better for him."

"Just so long as he feels better."

"You know him well?"

"Sure," I said. "He's just about my best friend in the world."

The bartender began drying glasses with a towel.

"You'd better watch out, then," he said. "Nobody can make trouble like a friend."

I said I guessed he was right. There were a lot of ways someone could make trouble for me, and Sebby knew every one of them.

14

Dr. LaRoche, who never volunteered his first name, asked me to have a seat in the patient's chair. His assistant had telephoned me that morning. The doctor had been contacted by a Nicholas DiBenedetto, and could I come by that afternoon?

How much would the visit cost?

It would cost nothing. The expense had already been covered by Father DiBenedetto.

Would it be possible to cancel the visit?

It would. It would, but there was the matter of payment. With such short notice, Father DiBenedetto would still have to be charged.

It was a move Lesch would have been proud of.

"How did it happen?" LaRoche asked.

He was holding my chin in his fist, and turning my face side to side.

"I owe someone some money," I said.

I felt that explained everything nicely.

"Ah," he said. "Father said you have a blind spot?"

"Off to the left. It's like someone's sitting in the corner, watching me. And I have terrible migraines."

"Fine," he said. "I'd like to run some tests for vascular embarrassment."

I looked around for his credentials.

"With blunt trauma," he said, "the capillaries become constricted. They don't deliver blood and oxygen the way they should."

"If you think it's necessary."

"You could lose your sight."

That seemed to settle the matter. LaRoche crossed the room and dropped the lights to a level best described as romantic. I heard him searching around his cabinet for a moment, perusing his chemical stockpile. After a few furtive glass clicks, and four hummed bars of *Carmina Burana,* he crossed the room to my chair.

"I'm going to put a drop of vasodilator in each eye," he said. "You don't have any work you have to do in the next few hours, do you?"

I said no, not really.

"And no driving," he said. "Look at the ceiling, please."

I did as I was told. LaRoche held the trembling point of the dropper half an inch from my pupil, and delivered a single

bead of clear liquid into the open trench of my eye socket.
The medicine was very, very cold, cold like it had been hanging out in the refrigerator for half an hour or so. Cold
enough that I was shocked by its temperature. I blinked hard,
and felt half the liquid run down my face in a single tear. It
hurt to blink. LaRoche repeated the step in my left eye, then
handed me a tissue.

"You must owe a lot of money," he said.

"You could say that."

"Close your eyes, and look at the floor."

I did. All at once I felt his hands on either side of my face,
and for an absurd moment I thought he was going to kiss me.
Then I felt his thumbs gently pressing against my lids, palpat-
ing to distribute the drops.

"These drops will dilate your pupils for about an hour,"
he said.

"Will my vision be affected?"

"Quite."

"How so?"

"Ever been to a film where they use soft focus?"

"Uh," I said.

"Romance," he explained. "Bodice rippers? Couples on
horseback."

"Terrific," I said.

"I'll need you to keep your eyes closed while we wait for
the drops to work."

I sat as quietly as I could. LaRoche did the same, though I sensed that he was counting the seconds separating him from his next cigarette.

In a few minutes, he said, "All right. Open up and let's have a look."

It was like studying a Seurat painting from a distance of one inch. Everything had dissolved into everything else, lines into lines and colors into colors.

"An hour of this?" I asked.

He swiveled the phoropter over on its arm, and fixed the scopes firmly over my eyes.

"What I'd like you to do," he said, "is look through these lenses and watch the eye chart on the wall."

"I can't see a damned thing."

"Good," he said.

I began studying the blurred white square at the center of my vision that almost certainly was the chart on the wall. LaRoche approached me from the right, a loupe in one eye, and a piercing white flashlight held up to light the way. He began turning a dial that switched, with metallic clicks, the lenses before my eyes.

"How is that?" he asked.

"Blurrier," I said.

"Good," he said.

After five minutes of this, LaRoche suddenly backed off, declaring my corneal circulation "acceptable," my red reflex "satisfactory," and my clarity of fundal details "all right." The blind spot would go away, he said. He pulled the mask away, raised the lights (here the world dissolved into viscous angelic soup), handed me a pair of plastic black sunglasses, and began to write a prescription.

"I thought circulation was acceptable," I said.

"It is. But even temporary disruption can cause permanent damage."

I asked what sort of damage.

"Photophobia, refractive error, field loss. Plus some arteriovenous nicking."

"Arteriovenous what?"

"Nicking."

He tore the prescription from its pad and handed it to me. I squinted closely at it and tried to decipher the letters. He'd prescribed Cafergot, a mix of ergotamine tartrate (1 mg) and caffeine (100 mg), for "incidental use."

"Take it whenever you feel a migraine coming on," he said.

"How much will all this cost?" I asked.

"Less than eye surgery. If you run out of Cafergot, just have an espresso in the afternoon. It's roughly the same thing."

"What if it doesn't go away?"

"We try something else."

"What have you got?" I asked.

"Oh, everything," he said. "Phenobarbital, fluoxetine, baclofen. But there are some drawbacks."

"Let me guess. They're expensive."

"Yes. Plus you have headaches, nausea, paranoia, et cetera."

"Paranoia. I think I'd like to avoid that."

"We'll see. If the blind spot doesn't go away, that's a bad sign. A very bad sign. Would you be willing to trade any one of these side effects for your sight?"

He walked out with me.

"I went to see your film," he said. "Did I tell you?"

We were standing at the curb. He'd come outside with me so he could have a cigarette before seeing his next patient.

"It's still playing?" I asked, astonished.

"At the Film Archives last Sunday. I took my wife. Father Nicholas suggested that we go see it. He said you were going to be famous in a few years. Is that true?"

"What did you think?"

"It was a nice change, having so many seats to pick from."

I was looking around at the blurry street, wondering how the hell I was going to get home.

"Right," I said, "there's a new thing where the theaters limit the number of tickets they sell, to make it nicer for the audience."

He took the cigarette from his mouth.

"It gave me vertigo," he said, "all the leaping around."

"Good," I said.

LaRoche had extracted a promise that I'd wear the sunglasses for one hour straight, indoors or out, to avoid what he called "corneal ascribement," which essentially meant that if I removed the sunglasses and glanced at a stoplight, for the rest of my life I'd be seeing a stoplight at the center of my vision. I'd come back to see him in a week to confirm that the damage wasn't permanent and didn't require an operation.

Too scared to take on the subway half-blind, I decided to navigate the blazing macadam. I couldn't have knocked over more than four or five trash cans. Once I walked into a lightpole, and at Fourteenth Street I was nearly flattened by a silent bus. I stopped by the Pakistani chemist's on the way home. LaRoche, providentially, had telephoned ahead for me. When the bill came, I couldn't read it.

"LaRoche dilated your pupils?" the counter girl asked.

I said that he had.

"Can I see?" she asked.

I showed her.

Big mistake. At home, later, even with my eyes tightly shut and the shades drawn, I could still see the bright wattage of her smile, the road flares of her incisors. I was all blind spots and imprinted images. Corneal ascribement, LaRoche had called it. Lingering things.

It was far too quiet in the apartment. After a brief search through the file boxes stacked in my bedroom closet, I located the spare drive that held my batch-list footage of Will

Thoreau, all the great raw film I'd had to cut from the finished workprint of *Prodigal Son*. I loaded up a longshot of
him playing a piano sonata and lay on the couch in the dark
listening to the soothing melody. Why hadn't I used this one?
It was so hard to remember all the tough decisions I'd made.
That trance, that waking dream, of editing. I still felt that old
urge, that need to go back and fix, recut, reconceive. Retake.
I'd run three thousand miles, but the urge had followed. That
was why Hollywood stank of thwarted escape. Because no
one ever really got away.

15

Than, Sebby's old assistant, rapped on my doorjamb. I had been at Axus for exactly fourteen minutes, and hadn't yet finished my first cup of coffee. I was feeling what the psych wards at Bellevue would have called "blocked" by the idea of being confined to one room, with the same view, the same perspective, and the same routines for an entire day. I'd never held a straight office job, and these first few minutes had reminded me why.

"Someone here to see you, Mike," he said.

He raised an eyebrow.

"Big guy," he said. "You want me to send him away?"

I sat back and noticed that I'd left mirrored ghosts of my palms evaporating on the surface of the desk.

I passed a hand over my face and said, "You'd better send him in."

Than left, and a moment later Popoloskouros occupied the doorway. His already considerable size was amplified by the claustrophobic dimensions of the office. He looked pale and tired, unhappy that he'd been forced to travel to see me. I didn't know how he'd found me.

I had to clear my throat before I was able to speak.

"You don't look so good, Nikos," I said.

Popoloskouros sat on the couch and closed his eyes.

"I ate a bad oyster last week," he said. "It won't let me go."

"You're the color of a canned clam."

He lay his head back on the couch. He really was sick.

"Why are you making me come up here, Mike?" he asked.

I had planned to spread the ten thousand around, a thousand to each of the bookmakers, in the hopes that it would buy me some time and save me from getting put in the hospital. But because Popoloskouros had come to see me, I'd have to give him all of what I owed, plus the terrible vig. Twenty-two hundred, which left me just under eight thousand to spread among the other nine.

Too little, I thought. Too little by half, and not a thing I can do about it.

"I've got ten points over what I owe," I said.

"I ought to be making you pay twenty points."

He shuddered and bent over for a moment.

When he sat up again, he said, "It won't let me go."

"I'm sorry you had to come up, Nikos. I've got everything I owe you."

"It makes me look bad when you are ducking me."

He bent over again, his features cocked in a grimace of nausea and pain, and asked, "Did you hear about Vato? The one who fell in the race last week?"

"It's a sad thing."

"It's a sin to do that."

"What," I asked, "break your neck?"

"He killed himself. Shooting himself with a gun. The priests are refusing to consecrate him, so the wife is not burying him. It is all being very unpleasant."

I picked up a pencil and pressed the trembling point against a sheet of paper.

"Those priests sure do love life," I said. "A man can't even shoot himself without feeling guilty."

"Everyone was being disgusted by the fall. And another jockey who fell is starting to talk."

"Which one?"

"The older rider. Vosgues. You know of him?"

"I know of him," I said.

"He is finding God after the fall, and now he wants to repent."

I thought of Thierry's superstitious habit of crossing himself. How little that had done for him. Find God? I thought. I doubt it. Somehow I think it happened the other way around.

"It is not the first time this is happening," Popoloskouros said. "The jockeys fall and they see death, and the ones who live are frightened. So they are finding God. Except this one is telling everyone that he is fixing races. He's going to get killed if he keeps talking that way. The bookies don't like a lot of talking."

I was drawing a cage on the blotter, a transparent cage with no way in or out.

"You think a bookie will kill him?" I asked.

Popoloskouros shrugged.

"If the people he was fixing the races for don't get him first," he said. "People are not liking it when someone is fixing a bet. There is too much money going around."

"I'm sure they don't," I said.

"Thierry is at the track every day now," Popoloskouros said. "Saturday I see him at Aqueduct, down in the paddock. He is carrying a Bible with him, no shave, no shower. The same clothes he slept in. People feel so bad for him they pretend to listen. But he is only bad luck. I go to him and say, 'You're bad luck, Thierry. Why aren't you going away?' Do you know what he says to me?"

I said I didn't.

"He says, 'I am here to be sharing The Word.' With him it is The Word this and The Word that, now. 'I was a blind man and now I am seeing,' he says. 'Where there was corruption there now is righteousness.'"

He grimaced again.

"I don't know, Mike," Popoloskouros said. "I am thinking that maybe he wants someone to hurt him. I am thinking maybe he did fix the race and cannot accept what happened to the other jockey. So now a screw has gone loose. You are seeing it in his eyes, that he is not believing all this he is saying about The Word. He is feeling responsible for Vato."

"We all should," I said.

"You should get out of the horses, Mike," he said.

"I will, Nikos."

"Really. You've got no luck. I'm in this business fifteen years, and I know bad luck when I am seeing it. I am making a lot of money off bad luck, but then the bad luck is passing to me."

"I will."

"I'm going to get out, too. My wife and I are going to sell the restaurant and move down to the shore. We could open a clam shack and have a nice quiet life."

"How did you find me here, Nikos?"

He seemed confused.

"You called me last night," he said. "I got the message this morning."

I dropped the pencil.

"Right," I said. "I thought I had told you I'd meet you at my apartment."

I walked to the bank with him and withdrew a cashier's

check. I really was grateful that he hadn't slammed my hand in a car door. A broken hand was probably what Sebby had hoped for when he'd made the call.

"I'm eighty-sixing you, Mike," he said. "As a favor. You understand?"

"I understand."

"You should be staying away from those horses."

"I will, Nikos."

I watched him walk away with his sad, sick face, then went back to the office and tried to work my way through the first of the four development budgets I'd been tapped to monitor. It was no good. I kept thinking about Vato and what he did to himself. Maybe Thierry really was waiting for someone to do the same thing for him.

I picked Beck up at Kennedy the next evening. She came through customs looking more tanned and happy than usual, rolling two cases of film equipment and going on about a baby the woman in the next seat had let her hold. I was all too happy to let her talk. For the last hour I'd been sitting in arrivals with my head in my hands. That morning I'd wired eight hundred dollars to each of the nine remaining book-makers, and had been waiting for some sort of response. So far my answering machine had been silent. I didn't take that as a good sign.

"How was it, Beck?" I asked.

"I got some terrific B-roll. Lots of stuff from Tivoli. Grandparents doing the Charleston, and such stuff."

"That's not bad."

"I'm going to use it to bridge that stretch before Lake Constance."

"That's a good place for it."

"I know you said not to touch it."

"It'll be fine, Beck."

There was an unfamiliar tightness in my throat.

"I'm happy to be back," she said.

"You missed New York?"

"I missed the film."

"It's nice you still feel so close to it."

The surest sign that I was done with one of my own films was when I no longer cared about it and didn't want to watch it anymore. As long as there were things to fix, bad cuts or flawed sound, I couldn't stop thinking about it.

"I think that's because I made this one for me," she said. "Isn't that funny? People won't go see it, and I don't care. Because I know it's good anyway."

I cracked a window and asked her to get my cigarettes from the glovebox. The first drag sent my head swooping away. I sensed Beck's silent disapproval.

"I thought you had quit," she said.

"I did."

"Can I have one?"

We were quiet for a while as Beck smoked and watched the traffic and thought about her good B-roll. Her wheels were really turning.

"Thinking, thinking," I said. "Us. How quiet we are."

For a moment I thought she hadn't heard me.

"I've got a favor to ask, Mike," she said. "I've been thinking about it for a while. Some good things, some very good things, have happened in the last few months. I didn't want to talk about it until it seemed definite. It's looking like Miramax is going to back a script that Kate Black and I wrote last summer. It would be a Looking Glass film, made with their cash. Small piece. We could shoot it all in the Heights, maybe sixty, seventy days. They seem to be willing to let us pick the crew we want. I was wondering if you'd consider editing it."

I adjusted my grip on the wheel. So Beck had taken the next step. Now the studio wanted her before the film had even been made, and she wanted to bring me along with her. The car suddenly seemed much too warm, even with the cold air slipping in through the open window.

"I'd be happy to," I said. "Very happy to."

"As a favor to me. And only if you like the script. I know you have your own things going."

"Sure," I said. "As a favor to you. Only if I like it."

Sure. As a favor to her. Charity was how everyone, even Beck, got a first big break, but that didn't make the experience any less humiliating. I knew a hundred editors who would kill to edit her workprint, and she'd offered the work to me. All because I was down on my luck, and because eight years ago I'd nicely cleaned up her first film. Editing Beck, I'd be making at least a hundred dollars an hour, with hope for a share of distribution profits. After I was finished, filmmakers from both coasts would be fighting to get me. This was how you beat Jay Lesch. I'd go back tomorrow, tell him it had all been a mistake, and quit.

"Stop by my studio, will you, Mike?" she asked. "I'm going to digitize all this so I've got a full batch list in the morning."

We crossed over the bridge into Chinatown, and I let her off in front of her studio.

"Are you going home?" she asked. "I'd like you to see what I've got."

She yawned so deeply I heard her jaw crack.

"I'll come up," I said. "I just need to find a spot."

"See you in a bit."

I circled twice and found a spot in front of the Emerald Palace. Three cooks in filthy white uniforms sat outside on the sidewalk, smoking and talking and playing dominoes on an overturned steel bucket. They watched with bland contempt as I dropped four quarters in the meter.

I should show up tomorrow, I thought. I should show up and ask her if she wants to come down for dim sum. She'll say no, but I should ask her anyway.

I took the freight elevator up. The door to Beck's studio was open, and from the dark hallway I could see inside, where all the equipment, including her spare drives, her DV tapes, and her flat-screen monitors, had been dumped into a pile in the center of the floor and smashed with a crowbar. Fragments of pulverized discs were scattered in a wide fan. The crowbar was still there on the floor. Beck was going through the pile quietly, turning the smashed pieces over in her hands. She had a look on her face like she'd just watched her dog go under the wheels of a truck.

"Mike——" she said.

"What's happened?"

"Look at what—look at what's gone."

"What's gone?"

"All of it, Mike. I had two copies. I had two but they got them both——"

"They couldn't have got both."

"They were both here, Mike. I was careful to make a copy. One on the drive, and one on a disc, so nothing would get lost. But they got them both. That and the edit decision list. It was on the spare drive. It's almost like they knew."

She looked at the broken pieces in her hands, her face gone blank. She was too shocked to cry.

"Who would do this?" she asked.

I couldn't bring myself to tell her.

"It can't have happened," she said. "It can't have."

Beck dropped the pieces she was holding, then stood up

suddenly and crossed the room to the couch. She lay down with her face to the wall.

"You could put it together again, Beck," I said, though I didn't really believe that. She had all the old footage, but she'd never be able to recut it. She would just be imitating herself, and it would come out all wrong.

"Beck," I said, "I'll help you."

"Shut up, Mike," she said. "You want to do me a favor? Just shut up. Because I can't bear to hear another word."

She was crying now with her fist pressed to her mouth.

"Will you sit with me, Mike?" she asked.

I didn't answer until she turned and looked at me.

"Of course," I said.

"Will you get the lights?"

I snapped off the spotlight and closed the door, then crossed the crackling spray of fractured glass and plastic to the couch. Beck lay with her face to the wall. I sat beside her and ran my fingers down the length of her hair. She smelled of yesterday's perfume. After a few minutes I noticed that her breathing had slowed and fallen into the quiet rhythm of sleep. For a long time I sat watching the lustrous square of moonlight, radiant as an LCD screen, on the wall above her, trying to guess which one of them had done it.

Follow the plumb line all the way down, I thought. Get right to the heart of it. You know who did it? You did. You killed her film.

16

Thierry came to see me the next morning. I nearly had a stroke when the intercom crackled to life. The damn Cafergot. It was like mainlining caffeine. I lay awake in bed all night, tense as an overwound clock, with a transparent ghost hovering at the edge of my vision.

"Let me up, Mike," Thierry said.

"Mike," he said, "let me up."

He sneezed once, violently.

"Mike, let me up," he said. "It's Thierry, Mike. Let me up."

I was sitting in the corner with my fingers in my ears, staring at the square of fizzing light the low sun had carved on the filthy carpet. Thierry went on talking through the intercom for ten minutes, then gave up and stepped outside to call up to me from the street.

"Jacobs!" he shouted. "Jacobs!"

I went to the window and pulled the curtain aside. Thierry stood in the middle of the brightly sunny street, a Bible held tightly in his right hand, his eyes red as road flares. I wondered if this was what Father Kessel saw in his nightmares.

I buzzed him in and drew the bolt on the front door.

He came floating up the flickering stairwell, looking like Death himself, as dreadful as Father DiBenedetto's crucifixes and dressed all in black against the spring chill. I noticed the first hint of gray in his wolfish stubble.

"I knew you'd see me, Mike," he said.

I was pouring boiling water through yesterday's coffee grounds.

"It was the only way I'd be rid of you," I said. "To see you."

He grinned, and I cringed inwardly.

"But you won't be rid of me, Mike," he said, "because we're one in this now, in this thing we've created."

"What is it you want?"

"Me?" he asked. "I want to help you. I want to help you change and account for what you've done."

And that struck me as funny, and sad: Thierry telling me to change my ways, when my ways were so squarely being changed for me. Thierry telling me to change my ways, when the whole thing had already been brought down.

"Thierry," I said, "you're too late. Everything already has

changed. I owe money up and down the coast. My friend lost her reel. Everything's already been changed for me. You've got to stop telling people you were fixing races, or things are going to get worse."

But he wasn't going to stop. He wanted something from me, and he would be back and back again until he'd got it.

"What does your wife think of this change, Thierry?" I asked.

He looked into the corner.

"She took my children and left," he said.

"Yes. And why do you suppose she did that?"

He seemed to cringe. This was a question his false faith couldn't answer.

"She left," I said, "because that book you're carrying, that Word—it's just something people use to try and make sense of things."

I didn't really believe that. Because you couldn't know. God had pulled a great trick by never showing Himself. It took just as much faith not to believe.

"You've got to pray with me, Mike," he said. "We've got to pray for poor Vato. He went into the ground without a blessing."

"If I do," I asked, "if I pray with you, will you stop telling people we fixed races? Will you do that?"

"Yes," he said. "Yes."

"You've got to promise me."

"I'll promise you, Mike. If you'll pray with me."

We knelt down, and Thierry, absurdly, took my hand. His palm was hard and callused, his grip tight and urgent. He was mad, gone mad, and I was in so much trouble. His free hand was on the back of my neck. He began to pray aloud, a litany he knew by rote, and it cut me right to the heart, thinking of Vato going in the ground without a blessing. As Thierry kept on reciting, I thought about how he wasn't ever going to go away. I was beginning to understand him, and what providence meant. For me, providence meant the opposite of what it did for Thierry, and for my mother. For me, providence meant anything but salvation.

He refused to leave until I accepted the Bible he'd brought. After he'd left, I threw it in the trash. I didn't need it. I already had the needlepoint on the wall anyway, and Thierry's red eyes, and the fading blind spot watching me from the corner.

I went to Aqueduct the next afternoon and found Thierry striding the parking lot. He was yelling to anyone who would listen, preaching with his fire-and-brimstone oratory. He'd been a corrupt soul, he said. He'd turned his back on his talent, had fixed races to gain wealth, and now he saw the error of his ways. Everyone who passed put money in his hat. He didn't seem to need or want it, and he was lighter than ever.

Now, more than ever, Thierry would have made a great jockey. He didn't look a hair over one hundred pounds. It was a terrible risk to be seen with him, but I had to talk to him.

"Thierry," I said. "Thierry."

He turned to squint at me in the low April sun. When he said my name his voice wavered, and I realized that he was terrified of me.

"You promised me, Thierry," I said. "Remember?"

He nodded, and passed a hand over his face.

"I'm cold," he said.

"I'll buy you some coffee," I said.

I drove him to a diner, where I ordered each of us a plate of eggs and ham. As we waited we sat watching each other, Thierry with his hands wrapped around his coffee mug.

"You've got to stop this, Thierry," I said. "One person's already got killed. You're going to be next. I'm begging you. I'm begging you to stop."

He grinned at me, a big empty shark's grin.

"But it's not me who's confessing, Mike," he said. "It's not me doing the talking. How am I to stop providence when it isn't me doing the talking?"

"There is no voice, Thierry," I said. "There's only you. You've gone mad with guilt. You're just listening to the white noise in your head."

I had seen what death did to the people it left behind. I had watched my grandparents grow old and expire from cancer, from time, from days lived, and had seen what happened to my parents after that. At its extremes, grief began to re-semble madness. Because there was no getting around the fact that the dead were going to stay that way forever.

The waitress brought our food, and we both sat and watched it turn cold.

As we were walking out to my car, I noticed a brick lying on the ground by my rear fender, and I wondered, Well, why not? No one's around to see me do it. No one would miss him. He'd be better off.

But I was too afraid of him.

Because if I tried to do it—

If I went for him, and he turned to me, if he turned those red eyes on me—

If he looked at me with those red eyes, my guts would turn to water, and I'd run like I was running from God Himself.

17

I cut myself in two places shaving while I was getting ready for Lesch's birthday party and spent half an hour getting it to stop. Fucking Cafergot. By the time I found the Band-aids the blood was everywhere, running down my chin and dripping through my cupped hands onto the tile floor. I had to shift gears and go through the cabinets looking for something heavier, a towel or a rag to stop it. By the time I'd got it stopped the bathroom looked like a set from a splatter flick.

I was half an hour late. There looked to be at least seventy people in Lesch's townhouse, Hollywood transplants with designer tans, most of them crammed into the first-floor library. I didn't recognize a single person. I was negotiating a route to the bar when all at once the lights went black and the music cut out. In the downbeat of silence that followed, Lesch swore eloquently, and Gina, from the kitchen, called out, "It was the blender, Jay." He went downstairs, and we waited in darkness and listened with a fair share of amusement as he banged around through the basement, cursing a black stream as he tripped and sprawled his way to the fuse box.

The first thing I saw when the lights came up was Sebby. He'd materialized, with apparitionlike suddenness, across the doorway from me, and was searching the crowd. He grinned at me as he saw me coming toward him.

"Hi, Mike," he said. "How's Beck?"

I hit him as hard as I could. I damn near broke my hand on his face and I didn't care. It was the first punch I'd ever thrown in anger. I'd been in fights before, but I'd never thrown a punch with anything behind it but fear. He never even had time to put his hands up. The punch caught him square in the face and put him down. With the first punch the anger came boiling up, and I only wanted to give him another. Sebby was on his knees, with one hand held up, as if to wave away any assistance offered. I was trying to get to him. I was trying to get to him, but I couldn't. Someone was pulling at my collar, holding me back. One of the buttons on my shirt let go, I was trying so hard to get to him. I felt that I had to get to him to give him another before he got up. That would put him down for good, so I could give him another and another.

"You lousy welshing fuck," I said. "You dirty—"

I could hear Gina behind me, calling my name.

"You welshing bastard—" I said.

Sebby was still waving away assistance.

"It's all right," he said. "I don't blame you."

I landed another punch on the side of his head.

"I don't blame you," Sebby said. "No sir, I don't blame you one bit."

An arm went around my neck and cut off my air. I was dragged back into the library. I couldn't see who it was that was holding me, but by the scent of his aftershave I guessed that it was Lesch. Sebby was still on his hands and knees in the hallway. His lip was bleeding where I'd hit him the first time. I was trying to get to him. The room had fallen completely silent.

"I don't blame you, Mike," Sebby said. "Not one bit."

"You lousy bastard," I said. "You welshing—"

He pressed his palm to his mouth.

"It's okay, Mike," he said. "It's just getting started. You'll have plenty of time."

"You'd better go, Sebby," Jay said.

Jay had let me go, and I was trying to catch my breath. My cuts had reopened, and his sleeve was bloody where he'd been holding me. In the back of the crowd someone asked, "What happened?" and another person answered, "Sebby must have hit him first. Look at his face."

"If I see you again—" I said, heaving breaths.

Sebby got himself up on one knee, then wrenched himself upright.

"I had to do it, Sebby," Jay said. "It wasn't Mike. You've got to understand that. I did it because it was what I had to do."

"Of course, Jay," Sebby said, holding the doorjamb tightly for balance. "You had to do it. I'm sure my father will understand, because, after all, we're human beings. But you don't do human, do you, Jay? I don't see how you could. Because you've got all the heart of a praying mantis having his evening snack."

"Get out, Sebby," Jay said. "It's your own fucking fault."

Gina brought me into the kitchen and pressed a rag to my face. The blood was all over my shirt by now.

"What was that all about?" she asked. "He never fought back. He didn't even try to stop you."

"He killed Beck's film," I explained.

"How did he do that?"

I took the rag away and looked down at the bright red swatch in its center. It was an expensive, handmade terry-cloth bar towel, and was embroidered with a stately GLJ at its corner. A drop of blood fell to the rag and spread into the fibers.

"It's never going to stop," I said.

My throat hurt where my collar had been cutting into it.

"Let me get a styptic pencil," she said.

Gina went upstairs and returned with a white pen. She uncapped it, releasing its medicinal odor, then held my chin in her fist as she studied the cuts.

"This is going to hurt," she said.

She was right. The pen stung as she pressed it to my cuts. It was almost worse than having them bleed. Jay came into the kitchen and watched Gina work on my face. Little coins of blood had dried on the expensive tile, a faint trail of garnet ellipses leading from room to room. The party had gone on without us.

"Anything I need to know about, Mike?" he asked.

"Not really," I said. "Anyway, I think it's over now."

Lesch shook his head sadly. I could see he felt bad about all of it.

"You've got a lot to learn about Sebby," he said.

It was long past midnight when I crossed Charles Street to my front door. The overhead streetlamps had been smashed. Such vandalism never happened outside nice buildings. And mine wasn't a nice building. Once a week, it seemed, I had to step over a pole-axed drunk to get in the foyer or repair the half-jimmied lock on my front door. I'd just slid the key in the lock when the doors of a glossy black Mercedes parked behind me opened. And my inner alarm, which was always looking for the mistake, the oddity, the thing that did not belong, told me, a beat too late, that no Mercedes owner would ever leave his car here. Four men emerged, one from each door, Clive among them. He came around the hood with a tire iron held lazily in his fist.

"Time for a ride, Mike," Clive said.

I was already trying to back up. But there was nowhere to go. My back was against the hard bricks.

"I can get it tonight, Clive," I said. "It's not a problem."

"I'm not asking, Mike."

"A few calls and I have it," I said.

I was on my face on the sidewalk, smelling my own blood. He seemed to have knocked my very identity loose. For a moment I couldn't recall who I was, or what I was doing here—the information wasn't there. I raised myself to my hands and knees and watched as four drops of wine-colored blood, each bejeweled with moonlight, pattered from my forehead to the sidewalk. I was trying to put a coherent sentence together in my mind. I was trying to come up with something I could say that would stop this, but the words wouldn't come.

Clive knelt before me and tapped the tire iron against the sidewalk. I looked up, and blinked blood from my left eye.

"Keegan has a saying he really loves," Clive said. "Rolls it out every time someone like you ducks him. 'The power of man has grown in every sphere, except over himself.' Fellow named Churchill said that. I knew this was where we were headed first time I met you, remember? A bowl of soup, Jacobs. That's how fucking sharp you are. And now I've got to sort out your mess."

"What do you want from me?" I asked. "Because I'll give it to you, Clive. Whatever you ask."

"If you'd gone quiet," he said, "it wouldn't have had to be this way. But I can't have blood in the car."

I looked at him uncomprehendingly. He pointed his keychain at the car and pressed the door lock. A hidden latch turned and the trunk hatch opened.

"Clive," I said, and wiped the blood from my face. My hands were sticky with it. "Please."

I noticed he had a St. Michael's medal around his neck—St. Michael, who'd been charged with bringing men's souls to judgment. How Father Kessel had admired him.

"The trunk, sharpie," he said. "The trunk, or you get another one."

I begged, I pleaded, I told him I had a mother somewhere who loved me. I gave him everything I had. But in the end I got the trunk. I was still pleading with Clive when they forced the hatch down over me.

18

I lay in that dark space for what seemed an hour or more, feeling every instant the approach of claustrophobia and blind panic. For the first few minutes the car had queasily rocked, accelerating and braking, sending me into slick glides of nausea as we navigated the angled network of Village streets. The ride smoothed as the car entered a tunnel and then accelerated to what felt like seventy or eighty miles an hour over furlongs of straight highway. The trunk was small. I had never liked close spaces and though this was no coupe coffin-hatch I scarcely had enough space to roll over. It was impossible to judge the time in the dark. I thought of the luminescent green hands of my pawned watch, gathering dust now in its cheap windowbox. Sold for a piece of bread, and the bottle of wine it had got me was now so much groundwater mingling with earth.

Some time later we left the highway. Stones crackled against the undercarriage as the car slowed along the break-down, and the suspension began to thud and jolt on what felt like an unpaved road. I braced myself against the hatch and swallowed back the thin, sharp taste of bile. After ten minutes of washouts and axle-deep potholes, the car suddenly stopped and the passenger doors opened. I lay quietly, my body running with sweat, and listened hard at the outer night. I heard nothing but the light rain tapping the car's steel hull. Gradually I detected the odor of marijuana in the air, the smoke tinged with a sharp chemical-ether undertone I recognized immediately from all the ride-alongs I'd done with night-shift beat cops as a field producer. Phencyclidine, PCP, though it was called anything but that. Black Acid. Bel-ladonna. *Niebla,* White Horizon. The only drug that made even the juiced veterans nervous. Every cop had a story, and the stories were all the same—you hit the perp in the chest with three hollow-point bullets, and he kept coming after you. Like it was a fucking video game, and he was just hitting RESET. You did manage to get him down and cuffed? He ripped his hands right out again, even if he had to tear some tendons to do it, telling you all the while that he was Jesus Christ.

The hatch opened. Sharply cold air swirled in, and I raised a hand to shield my eyes from the light rain. Clive stood looking down at me. My eyes, accustomed to the dark,

picked up the phantasmal radiance of the silver St. Michael
medal at his throat.

"Out, Jacobs," he said.

"Clive," I said, "it's a few hundred dollars."

Smoke trailed from his nose. He flicked the last bit of the
joint to the grass.

"You made me look bad," he said. "Understand? My reputation. You can't put a price on that."

I clambered out of the trunk, felt the earth seesaw beneath me, and overbalanced heavily onto the wet grass. A
concussion? I rolled onto my back and watched the starlight
overhead smoothly double, then treble in a shimmering
pointillist grid. A concussion, yes. I got to my knees, breathing rapidly to maintain my equilibrium. The oxygen wasn't
quite getting the job done, wasn't reaching its mark. Off in
the woods I heard, as if in a nightmare, the sound of shoveling, the clank and soft shift of rock and earth, the rote cursing of tired men. They were digging a pit.

"Clive," I asked, "what do I have to do?"

His profile blurred suddenly against the starlight, then resolved itself. He was looking up at the sky, meditative and
withdrawn. He expelled a long sigh and closed his eyes
tightly.

"It's not me," he said. "You get it? I'm not what's doing
this. I'm not the force at work, here."

"Please," I said. "Clive, please."

"You don't understand," he said. "I'm not your problem."

He looked down at me. His eyes were all pupil. I could have dipped my hand up to the wrist in those eyes—it would be like dipping my hand into a midnight black lake. In that moment he looked wrong, not just crazy but *wrong,* the wiring in his brain reversed. Like the man on your block who talks to trees, has a microchip implanted in his molars, and says he can see in seven dimensions.

"You believe in free will, Mike?" he asked.

He drew a pistol from the small of his back. It was the revolver he'd shown me at my apartment, the stock and trigger still duct-taped. I went weak and vague at the sight of it. They'd leave it in the pit along with me. The blued lines seemed to glow with dark light.

Clive looked up at the sky again.

"I don't," he said. "I've seen too much of this. You're the same story I've seen played out fifty, a hundred times. You come into the bar. I think, Go away, go away. And you never do. At some point we lose the ability to pick what happens next. Come the end of it, every one of you is asking, 'How did I get here?' And you're asking the wrong question. It's not the how that matters. Fuck the how, Mike. What you should be asking is, why?"

Clive suddenly took a long step back, then cracked open the revolver and ejected a single brass-jacketed shell. He weighed it thoughtfully in his palm, as if appraising the weight of the soul it contained, and then tossed it into the grass ten feet away.

"Free will, Mike," he said. "It's the same chance I give everyone. And no one gets away. Not one of them ever has. They prove me right every time when they take it in the back. I don't want to do this, see? You know how badly I want you to get away? But you never do. You never do. Because it's already been decided."

"You could let me walk away," I said. "Wouldn't that be the same thing?"

He seemed frustrated with me.

"You don't get it, do you?" he asked. "How long would it take for me to find that round? Five seconds? Fifteen? Long enough for you to make that ditch down the road? Or just long enough for you to ask for mercy? How far is it to that ditch, Mike? Is it fifty feet? Or as far as the end of the world?"

I nearly overbalanced again as I got to my feet. Clive never moved. He was watching me levelly with those wrong eyes, those glossy pupils, and when his gaze flicked to the ditch, I said good-bye to myself. I thought I heard him sigh, as I turned and began to run, with equal parts relief and resignation. It was like running through deep water, running in a nightmare, with time stopped and all the world hushed, as if waiting with indrawn breath to see if you'd get away. I had run what felt like fifty yards when a loud report fractured the air, and something seemed to tug at my right earlobe as it crackled by. I ran to the right and fell, heavily slip-sliding in slurry mud, down into the ditch in a headlong plunge. Mud went down into my shirt, into my shoes. I lay at the bottom snared by thorns and slick swatches of minty evergreen brush, my elbows in a foul, still pond of rainwater. I heard Clive crack open the revolver and eject the spent shell, then load another in its place. He was weeping or laughing or emitting some hybrid of both. From deep in the woods the sound of shoveling continued. I crawled up the far slope, pulling shanks of grass, my clothes wet and heavy, and began to run through the birches without any sense of what or where I was running to.

After I'd run a hundred yards, I looked back. Clive had taken a flashlight from the Mercedes and was walking slowly up the road in the dark, pivoting the beam around as he searched the ditch. He seemed to have nothing but time, and was humming softly to himself.

I began to run and didn't look back again.

Then there was only me running through the trees, running and spooked very much by the idea of the darkness and wilderness. It was me alone, first running, then tiring and be-ginning to walk. I realized that I had got away from him and that he was still back there on the road looking for me in the

ditch. I understood. What had just happened was something
that was only beginning. It had happened because I had made
it happen. I had made it happen, and it was mine. Clive was
wrong, so wrong. You had free will. You could see the clear
moral choice at every step, and when you'd failed to make it,
you knew you were going to pay for it. That was why people
like Father Kessel were around these thousands of years. They
understood fear, and claimed to own its center.

After an hour of walking I began to see houses through
the trees. All were dark. I thought of breaking into one to
warm myself and dry my clothes, but decided the better of it.
Too rural. NRA stickers pasted on bumpers. Ten minutes
later I came to a newly paved road that bisected the railroad
tracks, a glow tipping the rise off to the right. I walked toward
the light, and as I crested a small hill, I saw that it was a new gas
station, the vacant pumps bathed in a radiant fluorescent glare.

The attendant had his feet up on the counter and was
watching a Spanish-language channel on a small black-and-
white television. He seemed less than pleased to see a muddy
and bloodstained man coming through his doors. After he'd
realized I wasn't going to rob him, he put down whatever it
was he had picked up beneath the counter and went back to
watching television.

"Where am I?" I asked.

Without turning to look at me, he said, "Vineland."

"What state?"

Here he turned. His total lack of amusement suggested he'd seen this thing before.

"New Jersey," he said. "You want I should draw you a map?"

"How far from New York?"

"Two hours. Maybe less."

I called Beck from the pay phone in the back. She was half asleep and not at all pleased to have me calling until she realized I was in trouble. Then she was calm and concerned and wouldn't let me go until I'd assured her I'd be all right.

"Where will you go while you wait?" she asked.

"I'll wait here."

"What if he won't let you stay?"

"Just come quickly, Beck," I said.

The counterman turned out to be a decent enough fellow after he realized I had money. He hung my jacket over the heater to dry. Within ten minutes my teeth had stopped chattering and I began to feel almost human again. I butterflied my forehead in the bathroom and washed off as much of the blood as I could. When I came out again, he gave me half a wrapped sandwich and asked if I liked to play cards. We played gin rummy until Beck arrived. She had pulled her jacket on over her pajamas, and I could see she hadn't so much as glanced in the mirror. She came straight to me, put her face in my neck, and wouldn't let go until I said I had to get to a hospital.

The Lenox Hill internist put four stitches in my forehead. As she gave me the lidocaine stick I gripped the chrome rail and bit down on a towel to keep from screaming.

Beck, sitting on the next bed, asked, "Who was it?"

"You wouldn't believe it," I said "You really wouldn't."

The internist selected a pair of scissors from the steel tray, leaned over me, and began to work. I could feel her snipping at the flesh. Sweat had broken out all over my body.

"Try me," she said.

"It was Sebby," I said, and we left it at that.

19

I woke from seven hours of coma sleep and found Beck sitting on the armchair opposite the couch, gripping a mug of mint tea. She was dressed in her robe, and was studying me with the same analytical look that she wore whenever she watched either a very good or a very bad film. It made me plenty uncomfortable. I feared she'd connected what had happened to me and what had happened at her studio.

"My hero," I said.

She didn't bite.

"I should think," I said, "that I'd be the one with a lot on his mind."

"I guess we both have a lot to think about."

"I doubt it will do either of us much good."

"But I can't stop," she said. "I just can't stop. Ever since that night at the studio. It's all I do now. Just think and think and think, and add new questions to the pile. I can't seem to find the answers I need to get past it."

"I don't know if the answers are there."

I sat up and rubbed my eyes gently with my palms. It hurt plenty when the stitches pulled. Everything hurt.

"Do you think I've missed out on things?" she asked.

"What sort of things?" I asked.

"The sort of things other women have."

"What," I asked, "you mean like kids and such?"

"Like kids and such. Yes."

"There must be a reason you didn't have them."

I said this partly because I'd sometimes wondered why I didn't have the same things other people had. There didn't seem to be a reason.

"I don't know," she said. "It wasn't because I didn't want them. I thought about it a lot. But there always seemed to be something else to get done first. Now I'm thirty-seven, and you read all these terrible things about women who wait too long and then can't. I wonder if I'm going to become one of those. I wonder if I already am one of those. All because I always had something to get done first."

"That's as good a reason as any. You have a lot to show for it."

"It seems sad, though, doesn't it? That what's happened is an accident. Even with my film. Maybe it was a sign. Maybe there was something good in it, what happened."

"Don't say that. Don't assign meaning to it. You don't mean that."

"Still," she said. "It reminded me that I might have lived my life another way. I might have come at it differently."

She was looking right through me.

"I wonder sometimes if it was worth it," she said. "It was all very nice while it was happening. There was a time when I thought it was shameful to care about anything but film. Now that seems so—juvenile. An egomaniac's daydream."

"It's not too late, Beck," I said. "There's plenty of time for you."

"Thirty-seven, Mike."

"That's not so old."

She gave me a wry smile.

"You don't believe that," she said. "You know how it happens. First you bargain. Then you borrow. Then you lose."

"You're still young. You can still have all that."

She set her cup down. She'd never lost that analytical look.

"Did you ever think anything would happen between us?" she asked.

She didn't seem embarrassed to ask such a direct question. I tried to be equally direct.

"Of course I did," I said. "I probably thought about it more than you did."

"I did, sometimes. Even when I was with someone else, a little piece of me was always curious about you. Now I wonder why nothing happened. I can't seem to recall what was stopping us."

"It's like you said. There was always someone else. Always something else to get done."

"Was I too difficult?"

"It had as much to do with me."

But she wasn't listening. That famous resolve had fallen to pieces.

"It was me," she said. "It's always been me, with everyone. They reach for me, and I'm not there. I was too difficult. I was too caught up in myself and everything I wanted to do. I had too much to prove."

"Anyone would have been lucky to have you."

"Not that way. I never made room for anyone. You have to make room for people. If you don't make room for them, you're just using them, taking what you need from them and not giving anything back. I had always saved that part of myself for my films. And look what it's cost me."

"It's your film that's making you sad. Don't do this to yourself."

But again she wasn't listening. She was talking to herself.

"I never made room for people," she said derisively. "My mother was right."

She angrily swiped away her tears and stood up.

"I'm going to make another," she said. "Do you want one?"

But she waited there for a moment, looking defeated and spent, her red-rimmed eyes fixed on me, and gradually I became aware that she was wearing nothing under her robe. There was nothing coquettish or cheap in her frank posture. It was only as if she had acknowledged her athletic beauty, her natural grace. All that separated me from her was the thin fabric, and she wanted me to know that. She wanted me to want her, and I did. But I'd stolen from her, and had killed the thing she loved the most. The only genuine feeling I could register was my own gutlessness.

As the silence lengthened, her face and neck began to flush with humiliation and shame. I was humiliated for her.

Oh, Christ, I thought. Oh, Beck.

I turned away from her. A moment later I heard the click of her teacup against the surface of the coffee table, and the hushed sibilant of the fabric of her robe. As she climbed in under the sheet with me she shivered once, just once—a long tremor that juddered the length of her body. A shiver of surrender. I felt the cool loveliness of her skin against me, the long Scandinavian build, the cold points of her nipples against the liquid softness of her breasts. She knew I couldn't refuse her. I had humiliated her, and she had turned the humiliation aside in the surest way she knew.

"You understand, don't you, Mike?" she asked.

Her hands were stroking my hair, my neck, and I felt, in that instant, how alike violence and intimacy were, how dreadful and vivid and hurtful they both could be. I thought of what Clive had said about free will, the clear moral choice. If you hadn't taken it, if you'd retreated from it, you had to pay and pay until the debt was closed. This was the price. She was here in bed with me, her skin against mine, a moment I'd dreamed of a thousand thousand times. But her touch registered, somehow, as pain.

"I do," I said. "I do, but I can't."

"Yes you can, Mike."

"Are you sure?"

"I'm sure," she said. "Turn around, Mike."

I did.

Oh, I did. I turned around and said good-bye to myself again. And for the first time in days—weeks or even years, it seemed—all the complications fell away, and I was at peace.

When it was done she lay over me with her face pressed into my neck, her fingers in my hair, and then she began to cry. At last she cried.

"My God," she said, "you must think I'm so ridiculous."

I pressed my hand to my mouth.

You no-good, rotten son of a bitch, I thought. You black-hearted son of a bitch.

———

Beck went out later that morning to meet the insurance agent at her studio. I stood at the window watching her pick her way up the street, then took her laptop and batch list drive off the shelf and brought them to her desk. I loaded the rough cut of *The Stone Jury* and watched it at quintupled speed with the sound off. Typically for Beck, the rough cut was extremely clean, all of it already there, and since I'd already seen the finished reel I felt confident I'd have the workprint finished in fifteen or twenty hours. It felt wonderful to be editing again. Within ten minutes I was working without looking down at the keyboard, spooling forward and backward in the footage, assembling and splicing. The physical act of editing, with its familiar rhythms. Months away, and nothing had been lost, nothing. I was reminded, for the hundredth time, that filmmaking wasn't an escape, the way everyone thought it was. When you were making it correctly, you brought everything that you were to the table with you.

Most editors liked linear machines, the old Steenbecks that used reels of raw film, because they forced you to view the unedited film over and over. You could go through the sprocketed film at any speed you wanted, at ten times speed, the action liquid and slippery as mercury, with each frame 1/240 of a second, or slowly, frame by frame, as if turning a series of photographs over in your hands. You could even vary the speed, beginning slowly, the frames ticking by like signposts on a straight highway, and then going slightly faster, the pictures beginning to blur, until that startling moment when the miracle occurs—the photographs come to life, and the motion begins to happen inside the frame. Moving pictures.

Every cut you made asked a question, the same question I'd been asked at seminars, at cocktail parties, in postcoital bed: How can you know for sure? How can you know what cut is right, what cut is good? What is the universal? How can you be sure? I always withheld the answer, not because I wasn't sure of it, but because I believed it would be wasted on anyone who had to ask. They didn't want truth, they wanted the shortcut, the charm, the secret. How do you know? Here's how: you make the cut, and run it by your heart. If your heart assents, if it doesn't object, you keep it and move on.

I worked for nine hours, and would have gone longer if Beck hadn't called up through the intercom to ask me to let her in. I collapsed the laptop and shoveled the drive back on the shelf before she'd made it upstairs.

While she was in the shower, I telephoned Jay Lesch.

"You were missed today," he said.

"It couldn't be helped."

"I hope there's a good reason."

"I'm not going to be able to come in for a while."

"Not this, Mike," he said. "Not now. I'm going under, here."

"I'm sorry, Jay," I said. "I can't come in. Not for a few weeks, at least."

He was quiet for a moment, perhaps to mourn the passing of my job.

"That advance," he said. "You've spent it?"

"I suppose you'll want it back."

"Keep it," he said. "If I'm finally rid of Sebby, it was worth every penny."

He hung up and left me to consider the smoking wreckage of my career. I was strangely unaffected. It all seemed terribly unimportant to me now. It was as Beck had said: an egomaniac's daydream. There had been a time when I'd thought that I wouldn't have wanted to live without film-making. And I'd been naïve, then, too.

Beck came out of the shower exhausted and asked if I'd lie down with her. After she fell asleep, I lay on my back watching the ceiling, listening to her still shape breathing beside me, then got dressed and went out to the kitchen, where I poured myself four fingers of bourbon. Bed, I should have been in bed, warm beside her, but I was so very far from sleep. I felt like I'd never sleep again. Had I been working on my own film, I would have taken the sleeplessness as a good sign. I always found it hard to fall asleep when the work was going well and counted the insomnia as a small price to pay. I could still smell her sex on my fingertips and, besotted with her, I almost went into the bedroom and woke her. The bourbon had hit me hard. To let her sleep, I had another, and at some point must have poured myself a third, because I found that the level in the bottle had dropped precipitously. Christ, I didn't even like the booze anymore. All it did was sort me out.

I woke early the next morning. Beck had already gone. I was excruciatingly thirsty, hangover-sick, and went to the kitchen, where I drank with my head bent to the tap. She'd left me a simple note on the kitchen counter.

I hope you'll be here when I get back.

I couldn't bring myself to touch it. I left it where it was and went to her desk with her laptop. I worked for another seven hours and had the sound synched by five o'clock. It was done, and, like my father's bolts, even God Himself couldn't have divined the difference between the two. The disc was burned by six. I placed it on the center of the coffee table with a note taped to the front.

I can't be here to watch it with you. Things are not what they seem. Do you remember when you taught me this one? *Det er for sent at lære at svømme når vandet*

når dig til læberne. I understand, now. "It's too late to learn to swim when the water is up to your lips." I'm sorry, Beck.

I left, and locked the door behind me as I went. I had no key to get back in. It really didn't matter, since I wasn't coming back.

20

Thierry received me at the door with a Bible in one hand. His wife, he said, had taken the kids to her mother's house in Alabama. She'd left him their newly built Tudor, but its semi-opulence had fallen into squalor since she'd gone, the bloom of spring gone berserk in the hedges, the bird feeder a dud promise. By the rank odor, I guessed that he hadn't bathed since the day she left, and I wondered whether the scripture had anything to say about cleanliness. It was another one of those sunny, weirdly cold spring days, and he'd wrapped newspapers inside his shirt to keep warm. He invited me inside. The utilities, he explained, had been shut off. By whom? I asked. By the idolaters, he said. They know not what they are. He prophesied his revenge, restating his belief that he was an omen of gathering providence. There in the kitchen he looked very much like the coming of one thing or another, but certainly not the coming of the Lord. He looked more like the coming of the other thing.

"You're falling apart, Thierry," I said.

He gave me that empty grin.

"What's the point of this, Thierry?" I asked. "What does it get you?"

"It gets me right with God."

"I suppose, then, that you and I want the same thing."

He asked what that would be. I looked around for a drink.

For Christ's sake, I thought. Don't pretend that you're not going to do this. Don't bargain with yourself. You walked your way out of the woods, yes. You had Beck in your bed. You can get the rest of the money you owe from your father. But have the sense to know the difference between an escape and a temporary reprieve.

"We both feel sick about Vato," I said. "For what happened to him, and for what he had to do to solve the problem. We both want to take away his pain, but we can't, because he's gone now."

"It's a sin, taking your life that way."

"He should have listened to you, Thierry."

"If he had, he might still be alive. If he'd found providence, the way I did, he'd have understood that it's not for you to decide the end, but for God to giveth and taketh away in His own time, and by His own hand."

He crossed himself again, and I thought of Popolo-skouros's *defixiones,* his curse. A curse—which was really just the business end of someone else's prayers, the wrong end of the lightning.

"You're right, Thierry," I said. "He should have listened."

Thierry was weeping now.

"He should have listened," he said. "Poor Vato. And now my wife and little ones gone."

"We can still make it right, Thierry."

"The only thing that can make it right is providence."

"That's right, Thierry," I said. "We're going to make everything right. We're going to use"—it was hard to say it—"we're going to use providence to do it. To make things right."

"Do you believe in the power of providence?" he asked.

Do I? I wondered. Look at me. Yes, I believe. Look at you. Look at what providence has done to you, Thierry. Look at what it's done to all of us.

"I believe," I said. "But there are others who don't."

He looked at me with mute confusion.

"There was someone else—" he said wistfully.

"Who was it? Who was it, Thierry?"

I waited, my pulse hammering in my temples.

"Laslo," he said. "Laslo."

"Yes. Yes, Thierry."

"It was Sebby who wanted to fix the races."

"Yes," I said. "You remember, Thierry, how he came to see you all those times? You remember how it was he who told you to ride against the rail, to square the pack and hold Mother's Gate back so he could become a wealthy man? The source of the corruption. Tell me you remember, Thierry."

"I remember."

"It was Sebby, wasn't it?"

"It was Sebby. He was the source of all this."

"You've got to bring him providence. You've got to help him in this life, or he'll pay in the next, like Vato. Into the ground, unconsecrated. Think of that."

Thierry was weeping again.

"But how?" he asked.

"You'll have to tell everyone," I said. "You'll have to let everyone know that it was Sebby who brought you to water and forced you to drink. You'll have to tell everyone how it was Sebby who killed Vato, when he told you to fix those races. Vato getting killed, that was really just a sign, wasn't it? Just another sign, Thierry, like the number six horse. It was righteousness condemning something that was unclean."

"It was unclean. And now poor Vato is dead."

"He is. And nothing will bring him back. The only thing that can bring about justice is providence. God's love."

"Sebby fixed the races."

"He did, didn't he? Because it was really him doing the betting, and not me."

"I remember," he said. "He fixed them all."

*

His eyes narrowed in righteous rage. It was there in Thierry now, the twin of that thing I'd sensed in Clive. A deep spark of malice seeking a target. It had found its way across the divide, from soul to soul.

"And now we'll make things right," I said.

"You've got to pray with me, Mike. You've got to pray with me that we'll be able to solve Sebby with providence. With God's love."

But I couldn't do that. I couldn't bring myself to go that far, after what I'd just done, especially when he looked at me with those red eyes. I got the hell out of there and went to the curb to sit in my car. After ten minutes I got my head together, but I went to pieces again when I looked up and saw Thierry there in his open doorway looking into the low winter sun.

I frightened a parkload of children, later that afternoon, as I was going for caffeine and cigarettes. I was crossing the hypotenuse of the crowded playground. Halfway across, I suddenly came aware of myself. Floating over the ground in my long black coat, with my long white fingers, my Bela Lugosi eyes, I was effortlessly parting those games of Look at My Foot and See If You Can Catch Me and The Basketball Is Mine. Activity stopped. A few kids had the courage to stare. One dreadlocked girl began to cry, her mouth describing a perfect little O.

I beat a hasty retreat to my apartment, where I showered and shaved, but made the terrible mistake of using eye drops to clean my contact lenses. Never do this. While I was in the coffee shop, the world began to assume a supersaturated, soft-focus look. The counter girl's piercings were as bright as light on water. I excused myself and went into the back bathroom, where I crept up on the mirror and stared at my reflection in disbelief. Check out those bottomless, dinner plate–sized pupils. Check out the man in the glass.

Who did he look like? He looked like Thierry.

My father messengered me a cashier's check for ten thousand dollars the next day. Production costs, I said. Interviews, pay-offs, greased wheels. DV tapes and location. I had the distinct impression, talking with him, that he wanted to give me twice that, he'd been so taken with *The Daisy Chain*. I wired a thousand dollars to each of the remaining nine bookmakers, with an extra thousand going to Clive. I didn't add any notice with his payoff, but the message was clear: *I am buying my life back*. Buying life, killing death. What we'd been in this for, all along. I wondered if I was worth that much to Clive.

Beck had left no messages on my machine, not wanting, I imagined, to make herself any more vulnerable. After I'd wired the money, I walked across town to her apartment and sat waiting on the bench across the street from her building.

How it must have felt for her to come home to that note. If I could just see her and feel some jolt of regeneration, some sense that by fixing her film I'd accounted for the pain I'd caused her—if I could get that, there was a chance for me, and for us. Because you have to feel that you deserve the other person. You have to be able to meet her gaze. If you can't do that, there's no hope.

At dusk she came downstairs, pausing to check her mail on the way out, then lingered on the stoop to check her cell phone for messages. I made no motion to go to her or catch her attention, because I could see by her expression that she'd made the connection. I'd implicated myself by fixing the film. It felt like the first honest thing I'd done in a year. Beck being Beck, she would have already made a peace apart from me. She wore that familiar look again, the analytical look I saw whenever she was watching a very good or a very bad film, and I imagined that she wore it all the time now, even in her sleep.

If that's the only mark you've left, I thought, she's getting off easy.

And people wonder why I like film.

Christ, what's not to like?

It's better than real life: rewindable, eraseable, redoable. Sebby's big, beautiful nightmare. All you have to do is snap your fingers and you wake up.

21

I slept no more than three or four hours a night for the next week. The Cafergot kept me in a round-the-clock panic attack. I was taking them three and four at a time to keep the migraines at bay. It gave me terrible shakes, especially in the morning. I never seemed to relax, not even during those few downbeats of rarified sleep that arrived just before sunrise. I had stopped shaving because I couldn't seem to do it without cutting myself. Cafergot was a blood thinner, and every cut ran for hours—the bathroom floor looked like a fucking Jackson Pollock painting.

I went out for cigarettes Saturday morning and found Jay Lesch waiting for me. He was sitting on the steps, dressed in a cashmere blazer that must have cost more than my car. I sat next to him and took a cigarette from the pack he offered.

"You didn't hear me ringing?" he asked. "I was at it half an hour."

"The intercom stopped working."

The intercom had stopped working, yes—but it had been helped along toward its demise with a screwdriver and pliers at four o'clock in the morning. The tangle of candy-colored filaments and quartz fuses that had lived behind its brass faceplate now lay knotted on my kitchen table. Because it was worse when you knew it was coming. I didn't want to know.

He exhaled smoke through his nose and squinted at me in the sunlight.

"I won't ask what all this is about," he said. "I think that's best, don't you?"

"I suppose."

"You haven't been answering your phone."

"There are a few people I'd like to avoid," I explained.

He rubbed the back of his neck and looked down the street.

"I've got some bad news, Mike," he said. "The worst."

"You have to get the townhouse rewired."

He plucked the cigarette from his mouth and watched as the wind stripped the ash from the ember.

"Sebby's dead," he said.

All the revenge I'd lusted after crystallized into despair, a perfect gem of despair satcheled deep in my chest. I hadn't meant for it to go this far. Not by half.

"When did it happen?" I asked.

"Yesterday. They found him out by the railyards. Someone beat him to death. It must have been those bets he was
making. He was in up to his neck."

He wasn't looking at me.

"There's been a problem," he said. "And they, ah, asked
me to talk to you."

I hope it was you, Sebby, I thought. I hope it was you, and
not me, who got you killed. Those other bets you were placing, and not Thierry. Because I could not live with that. I
didn't want you dead. I only wanted you to stop.

"His father isn't well enough to fly to New York," he
said. "They need someone to come to county and make an
I.D. I volunteered, but the father's insisting that you be the
one to do it."

"I've never even met him."

"Apparently," he said, "Sebby told him all about you."

"I don't—I'm not sure I'm up to it, Jay."

Lesch reversed his cigarette and mashed the tip against the
sidewalk, then snapped the butt into the gutter. He stood up
and brushed off his jacket.

"Up to you," he said. "I'm sorry, Mike."

"It's all right, Jay."

"I was trying to help. You may not see it that way, but I
really was. I knew this was where he was headed, and I didn't
want you to end up there, too."

He stood looking down at me for a moment, and then he

dismissed us, Sebby and me. With a shrug and turn, he said good-bye forever, and walked away. What a marvel he was. I watched him until he disappeared around the corner.

Can you live with it? I wondered. If it really was you who got him killed, can you live with it?

I took the train uptown and walked east across Thirtieth Street to Bellevue, where I stopped at the information desk to ask directions to the county morgue. It was strange being back at Bellevue after having spent so much time on the ward making *The Daisy Chain*. I'd been just about everywhere in the hospital, and knew the place as well as my own apartment, but I'd never once been to the morgue. The receptionist looked at me strangely as she gave me directions. I assumed it was because of how terrible I looked, what with the bandage on my head and the cuts on my face, until she stopped me as I was walking away.

"You're that guy," she said. "You were here all last summer with a camera. You made that film with the neuropsychs."

It was the first time anyone had ever recognized me as a filmmaker.

"I went to see it three weeks ago," she said. "My God, it was so good! I loved it so much I went again with my sister the next night, and she made my parents go."

"Uh," I said.

I was just beginning to understand what guilt did to you. I had never understood it until now. What guilt did was it made you a coward. Guilt made you hate your own face.

"It was just incredible," she said.

"Yes."

"It was so moving. It was so real."

"I have to be going."

"Could I get your autograph? Right here on my notepad? They won't believe it. They won't believe that I actually met you."

"Excuse me," I said.

I took the elevator down two floors and followed the corridor back to the morgue. The sign above the door made it very clear that this was not an exit. I pressed the buzzer and let myself in. The receptionist took my name and asked me to have a seat. She disappeared into the back and returned a moment later.

"He can see you now," she said. "It's been a slow day."

She held the door open for me, and I walked into a chilly room lined with clean white tiles. Four steel tables stood empty and glittering beneath the glare of two fluorescent lights, chrome blood gutters winking. The light seemed unnecessarily, almost sinisterly, bright. The pathologist, balding and owlish, blinked at me through the polished discs of his glasses. He was cleaning a set of chrome retractors with a rag.

"You're Jacobs?" he asked.

"I am."

He scratched his neck. He seemed intensely uncomfortable.

"Listen," he said. "I know this is our guy. The decedent. Some of these, you don't have to follow protocol. It's too much to ask. You don't have to see him."

"Right."

"But I needed you to come down. There's the matter of the writ. You can just sign it, if you want, and we'll pretend everything went down. The father wouldn't sign it. And he wouldn't release us to get any signature but yours."

He set the retractors down.

"In fact," he said, "it might be better that way. If you just signed."

"What did they do to him?"

"There was quite a bit of blunt-force trauma."

He seemed to pat himself down and then realized he was already wearing his glasses. He removed them and began polishing them on his shirt.

"A crowbar," he explained.

I stood blinking in the bright lights. It occurred to me that unless I saw him dead, I would never actually believe it was true.

"I'd better see him," I said.

He led me to the lockers, humming softly as he checked the locker numbers against the list on his clipboard. After a moment, he made a sound in his throat, set down the clipboard, and pulled open one of the lockers. Sebby was there inside, a sheet pulled up to his chest, his arms at his side. They had taken the crowbar to his face. His soulful brown eyes were open, burst capillaries plexed through the whites. All the light had gone from them. They were the pallid eyes of a dead fish on a marble slab. So this was Kessel's exalted death. Where is the glory, Father? I wondered, and felt my stomach fold in on itself, rebelling against the blighted odor of formaldehyde, the sight of human annihilation. I walked quickly across the room and into the reception area. The pathologist followed me, hurrying with his clipboard. I was fumbling with the door to the hallway, but it seemed locked.

"But the signature—" the pathologist said.

"You want me to get the door?" the receptionist asked.

Sweat broke on my forehead.

"Out," I said. "Dear God, out."

"I just need your digits, fella," the pathologist said. "For the decedent."

I scratched a line across the bottom of the page.

"Really," he said, "I'm sorry about this."

I went out into the hall and up the elevator to the lobby, then hurried past the receptionist, who called after me, onto the blazing sidewalk. At the first stoplight everything came up in an acid chaos.

So this was death. I stood there holding the light pole as the signal switched from red to green and back again, and spat in the gutter to clear the rusty taste of bile from my mouth. A bus came floating by, and for a moment I considered stepping in front of the next one.

Well, which is it? I thought. Are you going to pick yourself up and walk home, or are you going to step in front of that bus and be done with it?

I wanted to choose the bus. I really did. That would have been the honorable thing to do. But guilt makes you a coward, so you go on living.

Popoloskouros had left a message for me at home.

"Mike," he said, "you were always being straight with me, so I am trying to help you. There is a problem for you. Come see me tomorrow, because we are needing to talk. Something bad is happening."

And I knew in an instant.

"Thierry," I said.

22

He was there in the parking lot, scanning the crowd with his red eyes. The Bible lay at his feet. Sebby had been beaten to death, but Thierry had been left untouched. His madness had granted him a charmed invincibility. He was terrifying to behold.

Thierry silenced his oratory when he saw me. His life force seemed to abandon him, to drain from his frame and bloodless face. I wondered what I looked like to him, what I represented in Thierry's universe. I could guess easily enough. In Thierry's universe I was Death, come disguised as a friend.

"I knew you'd come," he said.

He began to weep. I wanted to cry with him—I wanted to take hold of his hands and tell him I understood. Because the sequence, the situation, made sense to me. Clive was right in that, at least. Forget how. Fuck the how.

"You've been telling people it was me," I said.

"Yes."

"But it was Sebby, Thierry. Remember?"

He shook his head.

"Don't you understand, Mike?" he asked. "It's the only way to get Vato's soul through. We all have to pay."

"Sebby's dead, Thierry," I said. "I'm not sure if you killed him or if he got himself killed. But I'm sure I'll be next if you don't stop."

His face split into that terrible grin, and the last fragments of hope left me—I actually felt them go. He was so very wise in his madness, this agent of right.

"You'll have to stop me, then," he said, "because what I did, Mike—it speaks to me in my sleep. It's so much harder after the sun has gone down. And there's only one way to silence it."

"Not this, Thierry," I said. "Don't bring it to this."

"It's what I want," he said. "You understand? I've wanted it ever since Vato killed himself. I was the one who loaded the gun for him. I watched him do it, to make sure he did it right, because it was what I owed him."

"It doesn't have to be this way," I said. "Don't make it be this way."

"It's what I want," he said. "I'm going to make you do it. You'd be doing me a favor, Mike. Can't you see that?"

"I couldn't. I couldn't."

"You did it to Sebby, though. It was the same as if you did it yourself, with your hand. And now you only have to do it to me."

"I didn't do it to Sebby," I said. "He did it to himself."

"I've got a pistol in my bedside drawer," he said. "A Sig Sauer with seven in the clip and one in the pipe. It's loaded and ready. I took it out last night and turned it on myself, but I couldn't bring myself to do it. I don't have the strength for something like that. They don't give you a blessing if you go that way, Mike. You need someone else to do it for you."

"It doesn't have to be this way."

He turned his back on me and retrieved his Bible.

"I'll be seeing you, Mike," he said.

"I won't do it, Thierry."

Here he turned, and the tired smile he gave me seemed almost benevolent in its simplicity, its tenderness.

"Mike," he said. "Poor Mike. You think you still have a choice."

I walked back to my car and sat looking into the low sun. I looked and looked at the sun until I'd burned a hole right in the middle of my vision, then lay down in the backseat and tried to rest, the sun swimming there in fluidly shifting patterns behind my closed eyelids. I wanted to sleep, to vanish into a well of oblivion, but instead I thought about the day we'd spent at Coney Island when I was eight, my parents and me. They had brought me on a late spring day just like this one, the pale sun nothing more than a ball of ice pinned to the pale sky, and near the end of the day I became absolutely determined to go through the funhouse alone. My mother was dead-set against it, but my father got her to relent. I bought my ticket and went through the slow line, looking back fearfully now and then to check that my mother and father were still waiting for me on the bench near the entrance. Then I passed through the turnstile and the darkness closed in overhead.

About halfway through I got lost. In every room they had those trick mirrors that turned everything inside out, with the walls warped and the lighting queered and shifting, and every so often you'd come up against a version of yourself that sent your heart into your mouth. I was just precocious enough to understand that I was missing the point of the whole thing. The point, as far as I could tell, was to enjoy the disorientation.

Sometime later I beheld myself in a room of mirrors that seemed to have no exit. I tried not to panic and went around the periphery in a slow circle, with my hands up against the glass, searching for the way out, but there was none. Where there should have been an exit there was only another me. I didn't know how I'd got into a room that had no way out.

I never cried out. Never once. Because I was afraid that no one was listening, and I didn't want to know for sure. I'll take lost over alone any day.

———

I waited in his kitchen until long after dark. I'd taken the Sig Sauer from his bedside table. It was heavy and oiled, and strangely beautiful in the moonlight. I'd held rifles before, rifles borrowed for the hunting trips my father took me on when I turned twelve, trying to make up for all that time we'd lost. We'd never killed a single thing—just walked over field and rock wall, winter lingering in the crisp weeds and dank mud, and if we ever flushed a bird or startled a doe we just watched it go, and laughed. I'd always wondered what we were laughing at and decided it was death, because mercy was the mockery of death. I was sort of crying as I waited, wondering if I really would be able to go through with it. Despite everything that had happened, everything that had changed around me and turned on me and gone wrong, I was still me. Even with the strange heavy Sig in my hand, I was all life and more life.

An hour later I heard a car park on the street in front of the house. A moment later Thierry came inside and walked to the sink in the dark. He filled the kettle from the tap and placed it over a burner, and as I watched the blue teardrop flames waver and right themselves I was reminded of the racks of prayer candles my mother used to light for her father. Thierry crossed the room to the stairs, but stopped suddenly, rigid and alert, halfway across the floor.

"Mike?" he asked.

He seemed to swallow the final consonant. As if to take the word back.

"I'm here," I said.

"You've come for me," he said.

He let out a ragged breath.

"I have," I said. "Because it's what you want. Isn't it?"

"Yes."

"Say it," I said. "Give me that much, at least."

I was crying again. I couldn't stop myself. I was going all to pieces.

"It's what I want," he said.

But something deep in those black pupils didn't want it—a faint animal glimmer, the distant signal of a creature that still loved itself.

He went for the stairs in the dark, as quick as mercury, too quick for me, and I put a round in the wall beside his head. There was a loud ringing in my ears. Had the kettle begun to boil? I got him once on the stairs, right in the back, but with phantasmal quickness he vanished into an upstairs room, leaving four ruby drops of blood on the carpet. I went after him, the air thick with cordite and spent violence, ice water pumping in my veins, and I found that he had, incredibly, climbed into bed, as if he believed that wrapping himself in the bedsheets would save him. The power of our illusions— I went weak just thinking of it. But then he raised his head to look pleadingly at me, and when I saw those red eyes in the moonlight the gun jumped in my hand, and half his face vanished.

Some time later, with the flies already circling, the sun just limning the horizon, and the kettle playing arias in the kitchen, I found that I was sitting on the edge of the bed, with Thierry's foot six inches away. I was staring into the rifled barrel of his Sig Sauer. Somehow the Sig had got turned around, and was pointing at me. The wrong end of the lightning. I had thought that when all this was over I would have silence, some distant relative of peace, but even dead, Thierry was still very much there. He was watching me from the corner with those red eyes and seemed, like conscience, like providence itself, to have nothing but time.

And I realized—I realized, staring into that rifled barrel, that you can't kill your conscience. You just can't. And once you've realized that, what's left for you to do?

But I'm not quite there yet. My God, not yet. I'll have to call Father DiBenedetto first, not Father Kessel but Father DiBenedetto, and beg him to send me home with my eyes closed, a penny on my tongue, and everything forgiven.

Maybe I'll never do it. Or maybe I'll do it tonight, because it's so much harder after the low sun is sucked under the horizon. The soul inclines to light, after all. If I can get the blessing, it's probably for the best.